Friends, Freak-Outs and Very Secret Secrets

I was panicking. It was an outside chance, but it *was* a possibility. Could Richie/Ricardo have decided he fancied me, now that Kyra had dumped him? Yuck: what if it was true? What would I say to him if he did ask me out? What would I tell Kyra? Oh, it was all too awful to think about. On my own.

"What do you reckon, Sandie?" I asked my friend, only vaguely aware that she had said precisely nothing so far.

"I reckon," she said in this wobbly little voice, "that you like Billy more than *me*!"

I hadn't expected that. And I didn't expect Sandie to run off right there and then, leaving me standing gobsmacked on the path.

Frantically, I wracked my brain to try to figure out what had just happened, but all my brain came up with was, "Huh...?"

Find out more about Ally's World and Stella Etc. at
www.karenmccombie.com

ALLY'S WORLD

FRIENDS, FREAK-OUTS and VERY SECRET SECRETS

KAREN McCOMBIE

for Yulinda, the tooth fairy
(amongst other splendid things)

This edition produced for the Book People Ltd in 2006,
Hall Wood Avenue, Haydock, St Helens WA11 9UL

First published in the UK by Scholastic Ltd, 2002

Copyright © Karen McCombie, 2002
Cover illustration copyright © Spike Gerrell, 2002

10 digit ISBN 0 439 95148 8
13 digit ISBN 978 0439 95148 7

Printed and bound by Nørhaven Paperback A/S, Denmark

10 9 8 7 6 5 4 3 2 1

Papers used by Scholastic Children's Books are
made from wood grown in sustainable forests.

Contents

PROLOGUE

Dear Mum,

I was out for a walk with Grandma today (well, when I say I was out for a walk with Grandma, what I mean is that Tor was there too, only he was pretending to be invisible, so we had to ignore him*).

Anyway, while Tor was trailing way behind us (I didn't bother asking him *why* he couldn't walk beside us, just 'cause he was invisible), me and Grandma had a really nice talk. About you. About you when you were a little girl, actually.

She told me about the time you'd cried when you found a dead mouse in the field behind your house. She told me how you'd decided to give it a proper burial, made it a little headstone cross out of two twigs tied together, and laid wild flowers on its grave every day for a week.

Then you got curious to see what was happening to it and dug it up. (Blee...)

She said you *really* started crying then.

Grandma told me lots of stories like that; stories that I'd never heard before. Maybe you'd eventually have got round to telling me them, if you hadn't left. (Oops – sorry. I'm doing that guilt-trip thing again, aren't I?)

But then Grandma told me something else. Did you know about this? She and Grandad had thought about having another sproglet after you, but they decided that they were so lucky to have such a lovely, pretty, perfect little girl that it would be greedy to expect more. Isn't that lovely? I told Linn that story when I got home, but she just grunted and said it was probably because they couldn't stand the thought of going through the baby-poo and baby-vomit stage again. I tell you, Linn's got a lot of bones in her body but not *one* of them's romantic...

Speaking of family secrets, I finally found out the whole story about my friend Kyra's mum. *And* I found out something pretty surprising to do with my best mate Sandie, too. Poor Sandie; she was doing my head in for a while with her clinginess – I mean, I could hardly turn around without treading on her size 37s – but I guess I understand why now.

OK, I'd better go – Sandie's downstairs waiting for me to finish this. *Pretty Woman* is on the telly (again) and I left her in the living room watching the end of it with Rowan, so there probably aren't any dry tissues left in the whole *street* now, knowing those two blub queens…

Love you lots,

Ally

(your Love Child No. 3)

* This stopped as soon as we got to the café in Priory Park. It's funny how quickly invisible people become visible again when they want an Appletise and a bag of pickled-onion Monster Munch, please.

Chapter 1

VIP (VERY INEDIBLE PIZZA)

"How do I look?" I asked, walking into our sunshine-yellow living room wearing a matching sunshine smile and my best T-shirt.

Sandie – number one in my Top Ten list of mates (erm, my list is actually a Top Seven, but that's not so catchy) – was perched on the edge of our big squashy sofa, brushing her hair. With, I noticed, the brush I'd just used to tug matted knots out of Derek the cat's fur. Still, I didn't tell her that.

"You look great!" she grinned encouragingly. "Really nice. You'll really make a good impression."

I hoped so.

In fact, everyone was keen to make a good impression.

There'd been a queue the entire afternoon to use the iron (and that's a first). The house had never been so hoovered (Rolf and Winslet smelt suspiciously of Shake 'n' Vac after refusing to move from the rug in front of the fireplace). Faces had been washed, cats had been groomed, scratches had been plastered after the cat-grooming (thank you, Fluffy), exotic cooking smells were drifting out of the kitchen (don't get too excited; it was Rowan's turn to make tea), and now all we could do was wait.

And the reason we were so clean and tidy? We had a VIP coming.

And the reason the VIP was coming to the Love household? Well, it was all to do with love...

Aww!

That's quite poetic, isn't it? Not the "aww" bit ... the stuff about love in the Love household.

You know, I sometimes forget how pretty our last name is. Love: nice, isn't it? Although I do remember the first time someone (a boy, of *course*) took the mickey out of it. That happened back in primary school, when this kid in Year Five laughed at me in the playground and told me that my last name was stupid and soppy and that me and my sisters and my brand-new baby brother (back then) all had stupid and soppy first names too.

This was pretty rich coming from a boy called Noah – I mean, it's not exactly Joe or Tom or something straightforward, is it? I said that to him, but he yelled back at me that it was in the bible so that made it OK; it was a *proper* name, not like ours. I argued back that if he was going to be like that, then he should think about the fact that my siblings were named after a loch (Linnhe), a tree (Rowan) and a hill (Tor), and that if I wasn't *very* much mistaken, God was in charge of making things like lochs, trees and hills, *actually*.

Course, my argument crumbled on two points. God's great at all that nature stuff, but I don't think he had much too do with the building of Alexandra Palace, which is what *I'm* named after. Also, Noah was a pretty thick kid, and despite being older than me he'd never heard of a loch. So he just went on pointing and laughing at me and I guess I lost that fight.

(By the way, I think the original Noah – who did all that brilliant saving-animals-from-floods stuff – would be pretty miffed that some obnoxious little kid's now got his name.)

But enough of Love the name, and back to love the *thing*.

I was still doing my sunshine smile (although it was making my face muscles ache) when I heard the doorbell go.

"I'll get it!" I heard Dad bellow.

"This is going to be weird, isn't it?" giggled Sandie, who isn't technically part of the family but hangs around here so much she might as well be.

"Yep," I nodded, resisting the urge to go and peer out of the big bay window at the stranger on our doorstep.

"Is Rowan nervous?" asked Sandie, following me over as I walked towards the living-room door.

"Oh, yes – she's changed three times and sent Tor up to the corner shop for more food," I whispered. "Something was definitely burning earlier, but she hasn't let on what it was!"

You know how some people are really dreamy, and things just slip through their minds like butterflies fluttering through a bush? Well, that describes Rowan. And then you know how there are people who are so nervy about stuff, it rubs off and makes you all nervy too? Well, that's Rowan as well, and making this special tea on this special Saturday night was bringing out the worst of both sides. Tor (the only one who'd been allowed within a seventy-kilometre radius of the kitchen this afternoon) said that Rowan had been doing her eye make-up when she'd let whatever was in the oven incinerate. And that she'd practically been *crying* over the burnt ... *whatever* it was when she shoved some coins in his hand and told him to run to the shop and get a couple of frozen pizzas for her.

I hoped the VIP wouldn't be too disappointed that his first-ever tea with us would consist mostly of cheese and tomato pizza and not burnt-something-or-other.

"Come on, then!" I grinned at Sandie.

I took a deep breath, stepped over a scurrying cat that wasn't Colin and walked out into the hall.

There seemed to be a scuffle of people – Dad, Grandma, Linn, Tor and Rowan – and excitable dogs barking and coats being taken off, which gave me just enough time to sneak a look at our visitor.

He was taller than I'd expected, and looked more nervous, too. But then you could hardly be blamed for being shy and nervous when your girl-friend's entire family has crammed into the hall to stare at you *and* there's a short growly dog chewing your shoelace.

In the kerfuffle and the noise, Dad suddenly seemed to notice me.

"Oh, and this is Ally, and her friend Sandie!" he announced.

"Um, hello!" smiled the visitor, who was obviously trying (and failing) to memorize all the names and faces while also wondering how he was going to remove the dog from his foot without looking rude.

Luckily, Grandma spotted his predicament.

"Winslet! *Leave!* Shooo!"

Three words from Grandma, and Winslet did as she was told. Like us, she knows that tone of voice means no messing.

"Come on through to the kitchen, Stanley!" said

my dad, in his best welcoming tones.

Our VIP shuffled after him, nodding at all of us in turn.

Behind his back, Linn raised her eyebows at me and gave me a little "Well!" smile.

I knew what she meant.

"Ally," whispered Tor, tugging at my sleeve.

I bent down close to hear what he had to say.

"He's got hairs growing out of his ears!"

I knew what Tor meant too.

But apart from the hairy ears, our first glimpse of Grandma's boyfriend seemed, well ... not too bad.

"This is…"

Poor Stanley. I could see the beads of sweat forming on his receding grey hairline. It was hard to come up with an adjective to describe Rowan's cooking, and Stanley really *was* trying.

Gazing across our big kitchen table at him, Rowan's face bore an expectant smile as she blinked her glitter-smeared eyelids at Grandma's new bloke.

"This is…" Stanley tried again, nodding down at the soup, "very unusual!"

I hoped his heart was all right. Curried lettuce soup wasn't to everyone's taste, but the thought did cross my mind – as every mouthful burnt its way down my throat – that it might be positively hazardous to those of an infirm disposition (i.e. an old guy with a dodgy heart).

"Thank you!" Rowan blushed, shooting a quick, triumphant "Told you so!" look in Linn's direction.

There'd been a bit of a fight the night before (or a "debate" as Grandma prefers to call slanging matches between my sisters). It was definitely Rowan's turn to make tea on Saturday night, but, since Grandma was at last letting us set eyes on her new boyfriend, Linn had decided it was far too important an event to let Rowan do her usual food-poisoning special. But Rowan was desperate to be the perfect hostess and wouldn't give up her right to cook. And, to be fair, Linn couldn't exactly do it, since she was working all day at her Saturday job. Same with Dad; he was busy in his bike shop. And if *I* did the cooking, Stanley would be sitting right now in front of two Findus Crispy Pancakes and a mound of Tesco economy beans.

Rowan would at least cook something more imaginative. Even if it was mostly inedible, it would give everyone something to talk about.

"Mmm, it's lovely, Rowan!" said Sandie, finishing her bowl of soup, while the rest of us still struggled to sip a few spoonfuls. "Got any more?"

Sandie's a delicate-looking thing – all big blue

eyes in a pale, heart-shaped face and with this straight, fine, fair hair – but boy, she must have insides made of reinforced concrete. She's the same round at Kellie's, when Kellie's mum tries to give us all this wild Caribbean food. The rest of us dip in, a bit wary of the really spicy stuff, but Sandie dives in on the hottest of the hot like she's never *seen* food before. I think this all comes down to the fact that her manically protective mum and dad only ever have the most bland and boring food. Round their place, everything's mashed, tasteless gloop. Like they're all eating *baby* food or something.

"Sorry, Sandie, there isn't any more soup," shrugged Rowan, suddenly coming over all confident and Jamie Oliver-ish at the unusually high level of compliments going around. "But there's plenty more food coming! I've made this brilliant tuna and nut pizza!"

Oh, no – Rowan had decided to *customize* the frozen pizzas.

I saw Dad gulp at that, but he'd never dream of criticizing. Usually Linn would (quite happily), but I guess since Stanley was here she'd decided to keep her mouth shut and nibble her way through the tuna and nut pizza like the rest of us.

"What's for pudding?" asked Tor, coming out with the first thing he'd said since Stanley's arrival.

Tor doesn't say much at the best of times, but having new people around makes him quieter than ever. Which is *very* quiet indeed.

Then I noticed something telling: Tor had pulled a hunk of French stick apart and made himself a doughy white-bread moustache (he had to swizzle his top lip into an Elvis snarl to keep it in place). It looked almost exactly the same as Stanley's non-dough, real-hair, white moustache. Obviously Tor was warming to Grandma's boyfriend. (Although Grandma would *not* be warming to *me* if she heard me calling Stanley her "boyfriend". That *really* got on her nerves. Dunno why.)

"Pudding is Custard Surprise!" Rowan trilled.

I saw Linn open her mouth and close it again, sensibly opting to avoid starting World War Three in front of Stanley. But I knew she was as alarmed as I was about what exactly that "Surprise" was. Knowing Rowan, mixed in with the custard could be anything from prunes to mince.

Poor Stanley. He didn't know what he was letting himself in for, getting muddled up with a family like ours...

"Well, Martin," Stanley suddenly began, addressing my dad with a hopeful smile, "you've certainly got a splendid family here!"

If I wasn't very much mistaken, Grandma was

cringing at that very obvious compliment. She's a lot like Linn; she says it like it is and doesn't mess about. But poor Stanley was only trying to make polite conversation.

"Yes, they're all right ... aren't you?" Dad grinned round the table as each of us nodded back at him – including Sandie, I noticed.

"You can certainly see that Rowan and young Tor take after their dad's side of the family!" Stanley continued, delicately pushing his unfinished bowl of soup away from him.

I felt mildly excited by that comment of his. I'd always thought I was part of the Dad Equation: the dark brown hair and eyes to match that marked me, Rowan and our little brother as spitting images of our dad. And up till now, I'd always been quite jealous of the fact that Linn was the only one that looked like our mum (and Grandma, for that matter), with her almost-blonde hair and colouring. But now, maybe, this stranger was going to be the one to walk in and see beyond the boring brown hair. Maybe Stanley could make out traces of Mum's side of the family in my cheekbones or something...

"And Linn and Ally look very like their Grandma!" Stanley finished off his observation – pointing first at my big sister and then at ... *Sandie*.

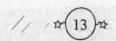

Everyone burst out laughing, including me and Grandma, as Stanley looked around in confusion, knowing he'd boobed somehow.

"Stanley, *this* is Ally," Grandma smiled kindly at him, and pointed to me. "Although Sandie is practically one of the family."

Poor Stanley. (Actually, that's always how I think of him now that he's become part of the furniture – poor Stanley, having to deal with our noisy confusion of a family after the peace and quiet of his bachelor pad.) Sitting right there at the table, he gulped a few times and went red as a beetroot (another ingredient of the tuna and nut pizza, by the way).

But what was funnier than Poor Stanley's embarrassment was how chuffed Sandie looked. I couldn't figure out which she liked better – Stanley mistaking her for me, or Grandma calling her "practically one of the family".

Either way, it didn't matter. Her spare (pink) toothbrush lived beside ours in the bathroom, 'cause she stayed over so much. Yep, I was as close to Sandie as I was to my sisters (closer, in fact) and I'd never get tired of having her around.

Or so I thought...

Chapter 2

SUNDAY WALKIES (AND SILENCES)

"Maybe he isn't coming," Sandie suggested.

"He'll come. He *always* comes," I replied, keeping my eye on the silvery white plane cruising by overhead.

It was going to … Santa Fe, I decided, settling on today's fantasy destination. I could be up there on that plane now, flicking through my *Rough Guide to New Mexico* – my dream boy (Alfie, natch) in the next seat – instead of sitting on a park bench getting splinters in my bum and a crick in my neck.

"Maybe he's forgotten," I heard Sandie continue.

"Billy won't forget. We do this every Sunday morning."

Yep – every Sunday, whether rain or shine, whether I'm tired or not, I trudge up to the bench Billy and I call home (around 11 a.m. on a Sunday, anyway), high up on the grassy banks of the park, with Ally Pally at my back and the high-rise pointy bits of central London off on the horizon in front of me.

By my side are Rolf and Winslet (the reason I *have* to come, rain or shine, tired or not). And either Billy will be here already, or he'll be on his way, to catch up and gossip with me, while his monstrously annoying little dog spends quality time driving *my* dogs mad.

OK, so Sandie doesn't usually join us, but she does know that's the routine. So how come – this one time when she'd tagged along – she was supposing that Billy wouldn't show?

"Maybe he's busy or something."

I stopped looking skyward and turned to look at my best friend instead.

"If he was busy, he'd have phoned," I said, wondering what she was getting at.

"Yeah, but maybe he's so busy with something that he hasn't noticed the time," she shrugged. "And that would be all right, because then it would just be the two of us and—"

"*Aaaaarrghhhhh!!!*"

Billy arrived with a roar and a thump as he leapt over the back of the bench to join us.

Rolf and Winslet found this extremely exciting. There was a general scuffle of barking and hairy paws as they jostled for position, both of them desperate to clamber all over him and lick his face. I was also pleased to see Billy, but didn't feel the need to lick his face. Instead, I just grinned.

"Can't you just walk up and say hello, like a normal person?" I asked him.

"Why?" Billy replied, blinking at me from below the peak of his baseball cap.

Fair enough. There wasn't a rule book around that said Billy had to act normal if he didn't want to.

"Is that new?" I asked, tugging at the cap till it came down over his face.

Billy had about a million baseball caps. Looked like he'd just bought his millionth-and-*one*.

"Yep," he mumbled from behind it. "It's Nike. Got it yesterday. Hi, Sandie, by the way!"

He waved at her, although he couldn't see her. Well, not till I pulled the cap off and tried it on for myself.

Maybe it was the fact that I was nicking something from his master, or maybe it was just the way Billy's hair was sticking up that frightened him, but Precious the not-at-all-precious poodle went into yapping overload.

Yappitty-yappitty-yappitty-yap-yap-yap!

"I thought baseball caps were out of fashion now," said Sandie, over the top of the noise.

"Dunno," shrugged Billy. "Don't care. Shut up, Precious! Go away! Go and play with Rolf and Winslet!"

"Since when have *you* cared about what's in fashion?" I laughed at Sandie.

I didn't mean it horribly, I just meant that she's the same as me when it comes to clothes and stuff – we like keeping up with what's in the magazines, but we don't exactly want to *shoot* ourselves if we can't afford the latest kitten-heeled *wellies* or whatever is "in". In fact, we are both guilty of sniggering quite a bit at some of the fashion junkies we see wandering around the shops on Saturday afternoons. You know, those people who look like they're trying so hard to be cutting edge with their clothes that they're just kind of *sad*.

Anyway, like I said, when I joked that Sandie didn't care about what was in fashion, that's all it was – a joke.

"Are you saying I'm not trendy or something?" she blinked at me, her vast blue eyes extra-wide and full of hurt.

Uh-oh.

"No, of course not!" I protested.

Wow, she can be *so* touchy sometimes.

Yappitty-yappitty-yap-yap-yap-yap-yap-yap!

Turning away from Sandie, I yanked the baseball cap off my head and stuck it back on the bonce of its rightful owner – hoping that might shut Precious up.

It didn't.

Yip-yip-yippetty-yap-yap-yap-yap-yap!

"What's *wrong* with him?" I asked Billy, staring down at the barking ball of fluff in front of us.

"I think he just wants to play," Billy mumbled, straightening his cap, since I'd rammed it on sideways.

Hat sorted, he bent forward and scooped up Precious in both hands, turning the dog round to face my hairy hounds, who were now stretched out and panting on the grass.

As if he had the brain of a battery-operated toy, Precious now totally forgot us and started yapping directly at Rolf and Winslet. I wished for a second that he *was* battery-operated – that way there might be a volume control on him somewhere that I could turn down.

"So, how come you're here today, Sandie? Just desperate to see me?" Billy grinned mischievously.

From the other end of the bench, Sandie made a little tutting sound and blushed silently.

Here we go – the usual way my two best mates communicate, or *don't* communicate, to be more accurate. In front of Sandie, Billy gets cheekier and more show-offy than normal, and that makes Sandie get shyer (and quieter) than normal. And that makes it really hard work for *me* – trying to keep a lid on Billy being silly and trying to drag Sandie into the conversation whether she likes it or not.

"Very funny, ha, ha," I said sarcastically. "Sandie stayed over last night, and just fancied hanging out for a while, didn't you, Sandie?"

"Mmmmm," Sandie nodded, keeping her gaze fixed on the three dogs playing (and, in grumpy Winslet's case, growling) in front of us.

"Yeah, my Grandma brought her boyfriend, Stanley, round to visit last night," I continued, keeping Billy up to date with the latest events in the world of Love. "It was pretty funny – I think he got a bit freaked out by Rowan's cooking—"

"No wonder!" grunted Billy.

"—and then, when Tor cut his pizza into the shape of a beard and moustache and tried to wear it, you should have seen his face! It was pretty funny, wasn't it, Sandie?"

"Yeah," nodded Sandie.

"And the poor guy – it turns out he's allergic to animals, and he'd taken this anti-histamine tablet to stop him sneezing and everything," I continued, turning my head to face Billy again, "but it didn't work – not against our zoo! He was snotting all over the place by the time they left, wasn't he, Sandie?"

I turned to face her.

"Uh-huh," was all I got for my efforts.

And so it went on.

Billy told us about football practice the day before, and demonstrated – in slow motion – how he scored the winning goal (see what I mean about the showing-off thing?). He told us about these three girls who hung around and watched, whistling at the lads and generally annoying them (a lie, I'm sure. I bet all the guys *loved* it). He even told us about the lad on his team who'd cleverly managed to stop a pass at goal by letting the ball collide with his *nose*, and how amazing it was that so much blood came out of it. (Apparently the girls disappeared pretty quick after that, looking a bit white-faced.)

The way Billy told it, with lots of acting out and exaggeration, it kind of made me laugh. Sandie? Well, Sandie didn't seem to manage much more than a limp smile here and there.

Maybe she wasn't feeling very well and just didn't want to say anything in front of Billy, I decided.

"Oh, and I forgot to tell you," said Billy, dragging my thoughts back to him.

"What?"

"Well, I saw Richie at football yesterday, and he said he wants to talk to you."

"Richie/Ricardo?" I asked, frowning. "Kyra's Richie/Ricardo?"

From what I'd seen of my mate Kyra's on-off boyfriend (currently *off*), he had all the charm of a doorknob. He might have tried to make himself sound more impressive by introducing himself as "Ricardo" to Kyra when they first met, but impressive he was not. Big-headed, self-centred, slimy ... yep, all those words described him well. At least, that's how he came across to me. Billy (who knew him as Richie, like the rest of the world) thought he was kind of all right. Which made me think that Richie/Ricardo is one of those boys that can't handle girls as *people* – only things to snog.

"Yeah, Kyra's Richie!" Billy nodded at me.

"What does he want to talk to *me* for?" I asked, feeling myself go pink.

But Billy wasn't listening; he was watching the situation that had developed between our dogs...

"Winslet!" I shouted, seeing what was happening. "Put Precious down! *Now!*"

Grudgingly, Winslet opened her jaws, releasing the grip she had on the scruff of Precious's neck. She'd been determinedly stomping her four stubby legs in the direction of the nearest bin, dragging a whining Precious with her. I could be wrong, but it seemed to me like she was planning on flinging him inside it – maybe after one too many attempts to sniff her where the sun don't shine. Winslet may be a strange-looking dog (a cross between something big and hairy and something with sawn-off legs), but she does have her dignity.

"Hmm, maybe I should take him home," mused Billy, as Precious bounded into his arms, away from harm (i.e. Winslet).

"Hold on!" I said urgently. "You haven't told me what Richie/Ricardo wants to talk to me about yet!"

"Huh?" Billy frowned at me, as if he hadn't the faintest clue what I was on about.

Hopeless.

For a second, I felt like doing a Winslet and chucking *Billy* in the bin…

"He makes me *so* mad sometimes!" I moaned to Sandie, as we strolled down the hill towards the park gate. "I mean, imagine not even *asking* Richie/Ricardo what he wanted to talk to me about – can you believe that?"

I was ranting. I knew I was ranting. But it's not every day that I find out a boy wants to talk to me (even one as obnoxious as Richie/Ricardo). OK, so I'd never, *ever* been in the position of finding out that a boy wants to talk to me. And it was freaking me out, actually.

"What does Richie/Ricardo want to talk to *me* for?" I wittered on, as Sandie kept pace at my side while the dogs bounded on ahead, barking at sticks, insects and invisible things. "It's *got* to be about Kyra, hasn't it? I mean, that would make sense, wouldn't it?"

My mind was racing so fast it was overtaking Rolf and Winslet as they headed towards the alley and the gate.

"Maybe he wants to ask if I know why Kyra chucked him that last time," I frowned to myself. "Or maybe he wants to know how he can get back with her. Yeah, it's got to be that, hasn't it? That would *definitely* make sense. Unless..."

A horrible thought suddenly slithered into my brain.

"Oh no ... you don't think he maybe ... y'know – likes *me* now or something?"

I was panicking. It was an outside chance, but it *was* a possibility. Could Richie/Ricardo have decided he fancied me, now that Kyra had dumped him? Yuck: what if it was true? What would I say to him if he did ask me out? What would I tell Kyra? Oh, it was all too awful to think about. On my own.

"What do you reckon, Sandie?" I asked my friend, only vaguely aware that she had said precisely nothing so far.

"I reckon," she said in this wobbly little voice, "that you like Billy more than *me*!"

I hadn't expected that. And I didn't expect Sandie to run off right there and then, leaving me standing gobsmacked on the path.

Frantically, I wracked my brain to try to figure out what had just happened, but all my brain came up with was, "Huh...?"

Chapter 3

GETTING CRAFTY (OR NOT)

By the time I got home, my brain was frazzled.

In order of importance, here's what exactly was frazzling my brain:

1) Sandie going hyper-space weird on me.

2) The mystery of why Richie/Ricardo wanted to talk to me.

3) The unthinkable idea that Richie/Ricardo might *just* be planning to ask me out.

4) Being angry with myself for even *imagining* that Richie/Ricardo would ask me out. How could I be that vain? He was *bound* to want to talk to me about Kyra.

5) So what exactly did he want to talk to me about Kyra for? Did he want my help? But why should I help a creep like him? Kyra was better off without him.

6) Wasn't she?

7) Should I tell Kyra that her ex wanted to talk to me? Or should I wait to find out what it was he wanted to say? (In case he *did* want to ask me out.)

8) But why *would* he want to ask me out? He'd never once been remotely nice to me.

9) But aren't a lot of guys like that? Don't they act all standoffish when they like you? (The weirdos.)

10) If I hated the idea of Richie/Ricardo asking me out so much, why did I feel so repulsed but strangely excited? And most definitely sick? All at the same time?

Urrrgghhhh…

I pushed the front door open and let the dogs tumble in, right over Colin and a cat that wasn't Colin, who were snoozing (up until we arrived) on the rug in the hall.

"Sorry, Colin," I called after the streak of ginger fur that was hopping away as fast as his three legs would carry him. "And sorry…"

I squinted at the huffy black and white cat, waddling away with its tail in the air. OK, it *had* a tail, so that ruled out Fluffy (no tail) and Frankie (who had a tail that bent over like a car aerial that had had a run-in with vandals).

"Sorry, Eddie!" I shouted after Eddie, recognizing him finally by his lacy ears (too many fights with too many cats through too many of his nine lives).

"Who are you talking to?" I heard Linn call through from the living room.

"Aliens," I muttered, walking through to join her and then flopping down on the nearest armchair.

"Oh, good. I'd have hated to think you were just talking to yourself," Linn replied, staring straight ahead at the TV.

Which was hard, considering Rowan was in the way, bobbing up and down on the floor.

I glanced at Linn, sprawled all over the sofa, and marvelled at the fact that she wasn't moaning at Rowan to move. See? It shows that *just* when you decide Linn is as bossy and narky as a big sister can be, she turns out to be quite tolerant and nice. Sometimes.

"What are you doing?" I asked Rowan, who was padding around on the carpet on her hands and knees – two dark, fat plaits of hair dangling down either side of her face – rearranging stuff that looked suspiciously like dried rosebuds and coat hangers.

"Making a mobile," she replied, holding up one wire coat hanger that she'd twisted into the shape of a heart. "See? I'm going to thread all these dried rosebuds on, then finish it off with a pink ribbon so you can hang it from the ceiling."

"Nice," I nodded.

It *was* a nice idea. And very tasteful, compared with Rowan's usual glitz-fest creations. But there were a *lot* of rosebuds and a *lot* of hangers on the floor. Was she planning on hanging them all in her room? You wouldn't be able to walk for battering your head on flowery hearts...

"Yeah," she smiled, gazing at her handiwork. "I know we only have to do one thing each for the charity craft fair at school, but I thought that it's just as easy for me to knock up a few of these – and that means all the more money for that poor little kid."

Oops. There was something else to add to my brain-frazzle list:

11) What on earth to make for this stupid school craft fair.

Not that the craft fair was stupid. It was a great idea, really. There's this girl at our school – Nadia Hussain – and her little sister has some really terrible bone disease that I can't pronounce, where she doesn't grow properly or something. Anyway, her parents found out that there's some amazing new treatment for it in America – which, of course, costs zillions – and her family really want to send her (natch). So anyway, Nadia tells one of her teachers about this, who in turn tells Mr Bashir the headmaster, who comes up with this fund-raising idea: a craft fair where everyone in the school contributes one handmade thing to sell.

Like I say, great idea. Only my hands aren't good at *making*. Anything.

"What are *you* doing for the craft fair?" I asked Linn, glancing over to where she was lying on the sofa, irritably picking pet hairs off her black jumper and trousers.

"Told you before," she replied, her green eyes flicking away from the stray fur and over to the TV again. "I'm down to do something for the food stalls. Carrot cake, I think."

I sighed. Everyone I knew was sorted when it came to what they were doing for the craft fair. Linn was cooking (I'm rubbish at that – no one was going to buy a bowl of cold, rubbery Super-Noodles from me); Rowan was making her designer range of mobiles (if I tried that it would just look like a bunch of mangled coat hangers); and Sandie – She-Who'd-Gone-Weird-On-Me – had already made a matching gingham apron and oven-glove set (snore ... I hate sewing and I still have the scars to prove it, where I once stuck my finger, not the material, under a sewing-machine needle. Ouch).

My other mates were all confidently sorted too. Kyra was making a mosaic mirror or flowerpot or something. Jen was sewing a rabbit-eared baby's hat made out of felt. Like Linn, Kellie was doing food – some spicy little nibbly things her mum had taught her how to make. Salma's brilliant at photography and planned to blow up one of her black and white snaps and get it framed. And Chloe was going to make a sculpture out of tins of beans from her dad's shop.

OK, that last one wasn't true.

But to be honest, I'd given up listening when my girlfriends had all been chattering about what they were doing, just because I was so totally lacking in inspiration myself.

God, where was Mum when I needed her? She was the queen of arty-farty things. You can't move in our house for paintings, drawings, sculptures and bits of pottery she did over the years. She never made it to art school (because she had Linn, and then the rest of us – and then left), but maybe it's just as well she didn't go – with any more of her artwork cramming the house, us kids would have had to move out to the *shed* to make room for it all.

I think Linn read my thoughts. Well, maybe it was the way I was staring miserably first at Rowan's sterling efforts then at Mum's stuff littered around the living room.

"Listen, you're good at plenty of things, Ally," she said reassuringly as I stared up at the big, mad, multi-coloured abstract oil painting above the fireplace. (Mum had called it "Skyward", and it was supposed to show a dove being set free into the sunset but I could never figure out which of the swirly bits was meant to be the dove. Doh!)

"Like what?" I mumbled, feeling sorry for myself. "What am I good at?"

"Well, what about English?" Linn shrugged. "You always get amazing marks for that. *And* History."

"Yeah, but I can't do much for the craft fair with English and History, can I?" I moaned, hugging my knees to my chest on the armchair.

"*I* could help you!" Rowan smiled up at me. "I could help you make something!"

Rowan's dead sweet, she really is. I know she was saying that stuff because she felt guilty about losing me my chance at a Saturday job recently, but then it wasn't her fault – what with the bullying and hassle she was going through at the time… Anyway, that's another story, and as much as I appreciated her offer I knew I'd have to come up with something on my own. That was the whole point of this charity thing – that everyone at school made a personal effort to do something to help Nadia Hussain's little sister.

And I *would* come up with something. Only it had to be good. And it had to be soon – the craft fair was only two weeks away…

All of a sudden, I didn't want to talk about

troublesome things like the craft fair. I had enough to worry about, what with Richie/Ricardo's ominous message and Sandie's mad act back in the park.

"It was cute last night with Grandma and Stanley, wasn't it?" I said, changing the subject.

"Yeah, it was," Linn laughed and nodded.

"Wasn't it funny, the way she kept blushing the whole time?" Rowan smiled, sitting back on her knees. "It was like she was *our* age, not sixty-whatever!"

"Maybe it never changes," Linn grinned at us both. "Maybe, when it comes to love and boyfriends, you feel just as awkward and silly and happy when you're a pensioner as when you're a teenager."

I liked that. It was one of the sweetest things I'd ever heard Linn come out with.

"We shouldn't mention it to her, though, should we?" I pointed out. "About noticing her blushing, I mean."

Honestly, our gran is *not* the sort of person that responds well to teasing. At the best of times. In fact, try to tease her and she gets as irritated and grumpy as Winslet. (Only there is a difference: Grandma doesn't try to steal your favourite shoes and *eat* them when she's in a huff with you...)

"Ooh, definitely not!" said Rowan, shaking her head and furrowing her dark eyebrows.

"You're right, Ally," Linn agreed with me (wow – that doesn't happen too often!). "She's maybe going to feel a bit shy and embarrassed about the whole thing. So let's not talk about it – apart from telling her that we all think Stanley is nice. Let's just all act really casual about it when we see her tomorrow."

Now it was Linn's turn to be right. And her words made me think about something – or some*one* – else. Maybe Sandie would be feeling a little bit embarrassed about what she'd said and done today, stropping off like that in the park. When I'd been walking home, my first instinct was to let her cool off for a bit and then phone her to ask what was up. But now I decided that maybe I *shouldn't* do that at all. Maybe I should let it all fade away and see what she had to say about it (or not) the next day at school.

OK, so it was a cop-out, but I could always blame Linn for the idea...

Chapter 4

INSPIRATION STRIKES (OUCH)

It was Monday morning (boo). I was at school (double boo). It was breaktime (a small oasis of happiness in a dull morning of boring classes).

Me, Sandie and Kyra were hunkered down on the steps that led to a side-exit door. We were chatting about the weekend (as you do), *without* mentioning Sandie's little outburst. *Or* the mystery of the Richie/Ricardo message.

The Richie/Ricardo thing: well, I *had* made up my mind to keep that one quiet from Kyra till I knew more. The Sandie thing: well, it looked like my decision the day before had been right – so far this morning Sandie had acted like it had never happened, and I was more than happy to go along with that. (Anything for a hassle-free life).

Anyway, there we were, yakking away, with Kyra telling us that her weekend consisted of bore-dom, Tesco shopping and more boredom. So I told her the funny story of the hot romance in my family, assuming Sandie would laugh and join in with the tale of Grandma and Stanley and the soft-centred grilling they'd both got from us all on Saturday night. Only she didn't.

Instead, she shuddered and said: "It's kind of disgusting, isn't it? The idea of old people kissing and ... *everything*."

I shot a puzzled look at Sandie. She was never usually so tactless. Didn't she realize that it was my gran she was talking about?

"Yeah, it *is* disgusting, isn't it?" Kyra joined in, resting her chin on her hands and her elbows on her skinny knees. "Once people reach a certain age they should be *banned* from doing any of that stuff."

Uh, hello? I hadn't realized my two mates had been recruited by the Anti-Romance Police. What were they going to suggest next? On-the-spot fines for anyone over forty seen holding hands in public?

"Well, I'm very happy for my gran, *actually*," I chipped in indignantly. "And I'd get a real kick out of seeing my mum and dad kissing!"

Meaning, I'd get a real kick out of having my mum and dad back in the same *room* together again. If only Mum would come home, I'd be happy if her and Dad wanted to kiss twenty-four hours a *day*.

But that poignant thought on the state of my family life went right over both my friends' heads.

"Parents! Huh! Don't get me started on *them*!"

Sandie huffed, scooping her fair hair back behind her ears agitatedly. "Mine are just *so* embarrassing sometimes!"

"*Some*times?" Kyra laughed wryly. "My mum is embarrassing *all* the time!"

Right then, the bell went and History beckoned, so that was the end of Sandie and Kyra moaning about their parents and ignoring me.

Humph.

"OK, people!" Miss Thomson yelled above the screech of chairs as everyone chatted and shuffled their way into our History class. "Before we get started, I just wanted to have a quick word with you all about the craft fair!"

There were a few groans from around the room – boy-sounding groans. But the lads responsible soon shut up as everyone else turned and stared daggers at them. After all, the craft fair was for a good cause. And anyway, if Miss Thomson wanted to talk about that for a few minutes, it meant a few minutes less of actual *lesson* time. (Hurrah!)

"Right!" Miss Thomson continued, once everyone had shushed. "I just wanted to tell you that Mr Bashir has put me in charge of rounding up volunteers to man the stalls on the Saturday of the fair. So, do I have any offers from any of you?"

Yes! I thought to myself. *That's my cop-out – if I do my charitable duty and look after a stall, I'll be excused from making anything for it!*

My hand shot up like a NASA rocket.

"Well done, Ally!" Miss Thomson smiled at me. "Anyone else want to follow Ally's noble lead?"

Noble: I was noble. Goofy, awkward or *worried* was how I usually felt. I hadn't ever thought of myself as *noble*.

I just wished I wasn't blushing so much – now a couple of the groaning lads were sniggering at me. Yep, I was back to feeling goofy, awkward and worried.

"Sandie! Terrific!" Miss Thomson beamed at my best friend, who'd just stuck her hand up too.

Chloe and Jen and the others hadn't joined in, I noticed. Nothing would drag them away from their beds and Saturday-morning telly – not even a good deed.

Then I saw Kyra's finger point languidly in the air.

"Kyra too!" Miss Thomson nodded, looking as surprised as I felt that Kyra was so charitably motivated. "That's great, girls – thank you. I'll talk to you about this later. But of course this doesn't get you off making your contribution to sell!"

Drat.

As my heart sank, our teacher wittered on.

"...and Mr Bashir is very keen to come up with any other ideas for fund-raising around the time of the fair, just to help top up the total. So, anyone got any suggestions?"

I don't know if everyone in my class was deliberately trying to waste time and postpone doing any serious learning stuff, but the suggestions came fast and furious. Pity they were all rubbish.

A sponsored swim? Snore...

A raffle? How boring was *that* – what would you win? Extra tutorials in Maths?

Asking pop stars to put on a charity concert? Yeah, like loads of pop stars would be at a bit of a loose end a week on Saturday and would fancy popping along to our school for a sing-song. *Not*.

"Yes, well, let's leave it at that, then," said a most unimpressed Miss Thomson. "Unless anyone has any final suggestions? Sensible ones, I mean?"

And then it happened – inspiration. In *my* head. What a novelty.

"Miss Thomson?" I mumbled, raising my hand. "What about letting everyone come to school in fancy dress the day before the craft fair? Teachers would have to dress up too, and everyone would have to pay a pound to do it."

Everyone was looking at me. Was that really

dumb? Was it as bad as Wayne's idea to have a
Year Seven versus Year Twelve basketball match?
Or Marc's suggestion that all the male teachers
should get their heads shaved?

"Fancy Dress Friday!" Miss Thomson announced,
giving my idea a name. "Ally, that's inspirational!"

Noble *and* inspirational.

Wow, today was turning out pretty good, for a
Monday.

Chapter 5

THE MYSTERY OF THE PINK FRILLY SOMETHING...

"Boys! They're useless!" I muttered, as I bundled the receiver down on the phone in my lap and stared grumpily down the stairs towards the stained glass of the front door.

"What's Billy done now?" asked Rowan, who was sitting directly behind me, a couple of steps higher up.

She'd heard the whole conversation I'd just had with him. Well, *my* side anyway. She hadn't exactly missed anything – not hearing his side – considering he was *so* useless.

"Nothing, *that*'s what he's done," I sighed, no clearer about what Richie/Ricardo wanted to ask me, since Billy had forgotten to find out at school that day.

Grrr.

"But what's he done to bug you?" said Rowan.

"Don't ask..." I growled.

And she didn't.

That's the nice thing about Rowan: she's

amazingly non-nosey (should that be *un*-nosey?), so, if you don't want to talk about something, she won't make you.

"Ally, is this Sandie's jersey?" asked Dad, all of a sudden walking out into the hallway and holding up a grey school jumper.

I gazed through the rails of the bannister at it and nodded.

"Keep still!" Rowan ordered me, slapping one hand firmly on the top of my head.

"Right, I'll just hang this up beside the umbrella she forgot to take away with her," said Dad, padding over the hall floorboards towards the coat rack by the front door. "You'll remember to tell Sandie they're both here, won't you, Ally Pally?"

"Why should Ally bother telling her? Sandie's bound to be round here for her tea again tomorrow night, isn't she?" I heard Rowan giggle. (Well, I *felt* Rowan giggle, since she was sitting so close to me.)

"Now, Rowan," Dad eyeballed her, "it was very nice to have Sandie here again tonight. And you know that Ally's friends are more than welcome to come here as often as they want. The same goes for your friends, too."

Yeah, like ultra-cool Von and grunge-boy Chazza would want to come for sleepovers and listen to us all moan about homework (our topic of discussion this Monday evening) over the tea table.

I *don't* think so.

"And did you notice something else Sandie's left behind this time?" Rowan continued cheerfully, as she yanked at my hair, twisting tiny little plaits all over my head. "Her dressing gown – it's hanging up on the back of the bathroom door."

"I'll tell her," I shrugged, then froze once more, scared to move too much in case Rowan tugged my hair hard again.

"Good, good. Um, what exactly are you two doing, anyway?" Dad suddenly asked us, crossing his arms and gazing quizzically up the stairs at me and Ro.

"Ally's hair's boring," Rowan announced.

"Thanks!" I huffed.

"Well, it was *you* who said it was boring!" Rowan replied. "And all I'm doing is trying out a new look for you!"

It was true; when Rowan, Sandie and I had been washing and drying the dishes earlier, I had whinged on about my hair ("It's not a style! It's too long for a bob and too short to be, er, long!"). And when Sandie eventually went home, Rowan had insisted that I let her play around with it for a while.

"OK, but why are you trying out this new look on the *stairs*?" asked Dad, shoving his hands into the faded denim pockets of his jeans. "Don't we have enough rooms and chairs in this house for you to use?"

"I was just on the phone to Billy," I explained, holding up the phone that I'd picked up off the hall table and balanced on my lap, with the cable still dangling over the bannister. "And Rowan wanted to carry on plaiting or whatever she's doing while I talked to him."

"Uh-huh," nodded Dad, sounding confused by the logic of Love children numbers two and three.

"Oh, and I just remembered – did you notice beside the draining board?" Rowan butted in, changing the subject *back*. "Sandie's left her watch here too."

"Hey – looks like she *is* trying to move in this time!" Dad couldn't help but grin at us both.

I know that it's a running joke in our family that Sandie is trying to move in to our house, bit by bit, but to be honest, that particular day I was feeling a little weird about it. Actually, I'd decided it was getting a bit *mental*.

Never mind the jumper and the umbrella and the dressing gown and the watch; when I went into my room tonight – just after Sandie went home and just before Rowan pounced on my hair – I'd noticed a pink frilly something sticking out of my top drawer. Now, anyone who knows me will tell you that I am *not* the sort of girl who would wear a pink, frilly something.

On closer inspection (i.e. I yanked the drawer open) I found a pair of pyjamas I recognized as Sandie's (the pink frilly something), plus two spare pairs of (clean) knickers, all neatly folded and placed beside my (not neatly folded) undies and PJs. Sandie seemed to be making herself a little *too* at home in my house, if you asked me...

Then Dad noticed that I wasn't smiling and presumed he'd hurt my feelings with his dig about Sandie.

"Only joking, Ally Pally!" he blinked at me. "Can't see Sandie wanting to give up being an only child with her own room for bunking up in this cramped madhouse!"

I wouldn't bet on that, I mused to myself, thinking of the pink frilly something and the pants.

"Anyway, better drag Tor away from the rabbits and get him ready for bed," said Dad, excusing himself and wandering off towards the kitchen and the back door.

"Dad was only having a laugh about Sandie." Rowan's voice came from behind me as soon as we heard the back door creak open.

"I know," I shrugged.

"So was I. I mean, I wasn't being *mean*, if you see what I mean," Rowan bumbled. "I really like her!"

Oops – it looked as if Rowan, like Dad, had mistaken my silence as a sign that I was offended.

"I know you weren't having a go at her," I tried to reassure Rowan, resisting the urge to turn round in case I spoilt her handiwork.

"Oh, good," I heard her sigh. "And, like I said at tea tonight, I really, *really* like that fancy-dress idea of yours!"

Rowan was obviously trying hard to come up with nice things to say now. She didn't have to, but it was still good to hear. Adding her compliment to the things Miss Thomson had said to me earlier in the day (calling me "noble" and my idea "inspirational"), it all added up to giving me a warm, fluttery feeling somewhere in the middle of my chest. Which I hoped was happiness and not the first signs of a terrible disease.

"If Mr Bashir *does* approve the fancy-dress thing, then I was thinking I'll go as a fairy. Or an angel. I can't decide," Rowan chattered away. "So, what would *you* wear?"

Great. Already I was stuck for what to make for the craft fair. And now I realized that my "inspirational" idea of Fancy Dress Friday meant I had something *else* to get stuck over too.

I suddenly wondered if I knew anyone with a cold so I could try and catch some germs from them and get sick enough to stay in bed both days next week...

"Watch out!" I became aware of my dad yelling along the hallway. "Bruised boy coming through!"

"*And* I got a splinter!" said Tor, coming up the stairs and holding out a finger.

"What were you doing?" I asked, inspecting the miniscule speck of stick in his pinkie.

"He was trying to check that there was enough bread on the bird table," Dad explained, rolling his eyes at me and Rowan.

"For Britney," mumbled Tor.

"Yes, for the pigeon," Dad acknowledged. "But the bird table was too high, wasn't it, Tor?"

"I'm too small," grumbled Tor, rubbing his un-splintered fingers over the developing red lump coming up on his forehead.

"So he jumped up," Dad continued, "holding on to the side of the bird table, and the whole thing toppled over and fell on him, didn't it, wee man?"

"Not wee; small," Tor corrected him.

"Well, come on, small man – let's get you into the bath and I'll see if there's anything in the bathroom cabinet to patch you up..."

As Dad and Tor stomped past us on the stairs,

inspiration struck me for the second time that day. (I'd have to have a lie down after all this mental effort.)

Tor being attacked by a vicious bird table had given me an idea.

And *no*, I *hadn't* decided to dress up as a pigeon for Fancy Dress Friday...

Chapter 6

MY AMAZINGLY UN-AMAZING INVENTION

I went "Whooo!" when I looked in the bathroom mirror in the morning.

I'd completely forgotten that Rowan had worked her Rowan magic on my hair. The little plaited strips, anyway. The rest of my mop was as messy as it always is first thing in the morning (like I've been in a hurricane overnight), but the eight or ten tiny plaits lay smooth, silky and well-behaved over the top of the tangled mess.

Automatically, I thought I should unravel my pretty plaits before I leapt in the shower, but something stopped me.

Pulling open the bathroom door, I strode over the first floor landing and tap-tapped at Rowan's door.

"Come in!" she called.

I stuck my head round the door and peered into her bedroom. It's still pretty in the daylight (pretty bright), with those raspberry-pink walls and all her mad knick-knacks and fluffy art all over the place, but it didn't look *magical*; not the way that it does at night, when she has all her reams of fairy lights on.

Now, though, it felt a bit like strolling through a fairground at 8 a.m., when all the painted machinery looks kind of harsh and garish, without those coloured bulbs glowing over everything in the dark of night.

Rowan herself was wafting over to her wardrobe. She was wearing her favourite silky kimono dressing gown (an antique thing that's full of holes when you get right up close to it) and had her hair pinned up with a pair of *chopsticks*. She looked more like she was going to audition for a job as a geisha than get ready for school on a Tuesday morning.

"Ro – can I wash my hair with these things in?" I asked her, holding up one plaited strip.

"Yeah – they should stay in through a few washes," she nodded, grabbing her school tie off the wardrobe door handle. "I tied the ends really tight with brown thread, so they shouldn't come undone."

All the time she was talking, I couldn't take my eyes off the chopsticks.

"Are you wearing those in your hair today?" I gulped, remembering that it was only recently that

Rowan had been bullied by a pair of bozos in her year for wearing all the eccentric stuff she did.

"Course not!" Rowan laughed, pulling a white shirt and a long black pencil-skirt out of the old wooden wardrobe. "I'm just pinning it up out of the way till I get dressed and ready!"

Phew. It had been such a relief when Lisa Dean and Tasha Franklin had given up their hobby of bullying Rowan; I didn't want it to start up again. And there was something about those chopsticks that said red-rag-to-a-bull to me.

"No, I'm going to wear my hair up and put these fake flowers in today!" she smiled enthusiastically, holding up two huge purple daisy things.

"Mmm, nice," I said through gritted teeth, then edged out of her room with my fingers crossed behind my back...

"You'll be dressing like Rowan next!" Chloe teased me, examining my hippy-ish hairstyle during the morning break.

"Yeah, you'll be coming into school in Chinese slippers and pink tights!" giggled Jen.

My friends regularly took the mickey out of what Rowan turned up in, but I knew they didn't mean it in that sneery, nasty way that the likes of Tasha and Lisa did. My lot maybe thought Ro was weird, but I knew they were also kind of fascinated by her and thought it was quite interesting that I had a sister who was such a space cadet. (As for Linn ... they're all totally in awe of her. Not just 'cause she's scary, I mean, but 'cause – and I'd never say this to her face – she is pretty gorgeous, in an uptight, perma-ironed way.)

"Pity you aren't arty like your sister," Chloe grinned at me, in that cocky way she has.

"What d'you mean?" I asked her, sensing more slagging coming my way.

"Well, what was that thing supposed to *be* this morning?" Chloe asked with a smirk.

I tried to quickly work out what she meant, but while my brain was ticking away I got distracted by Jen doing her usual Jen thing and crumpling into a fit of giggles. Obviously, I'd been discussed already.

"What thing?" I demanded of Chloe, who was smiling smugly at me. "What are you on about? Tell me!"

"Well, that thing you started making in Design & Technology today. What is it? Apart from a disaster!" said Chloe, while Jen went worryingly breathless, she was giggling so much.

"For your information," I said haughtily (though I was trying not to grin too), "it's a bird table."

"A *bird* table?" Chloe choked. "But it's about

twenty centimetres tall! Whose garden is it for? The fairies?"

That *was* kind of funny. Actually, that was so funny that I started giggling as much as Jen and now Chloe was. I was laughing too much to explain that the Windowsill Bird Table was my latest invention (not that I'd ever invented anything before, apart from a peanut butter and tomato sauce sandwich, which I was very fond of for about five seconds when I was little).

The Windowsill Bird Table was inspired, of course, by Tor's little accident the night before – but it wasn't just for kids. When it came to the craft fair, I was going to make a sign for this miniature garden-implement, explaining that it was perfect for people living in flats. Stick some bread and seeds on your bird table, bung it out on your windowsill, and – hey presto! – your local birdie wildlife queues up for its lunch, without the need for a garden *or* a kid-battering, full-size bird table.

Sheer inspiration. Even if I *was* having probems getting all the straight bits of wood to go at right-angles to one another.

It was while me and Chloe and Jen were hiccup-ing with laughter that Sandie arrived, having trotted along to the school canteen shop for a carton of apple juice.

When I finally noticed her beside me, her face was like a little worried triangle. Her blue eyes were huge in her pale face, which tapered down to this weeny rosebud-mouth sucking at a straw – and she was staring round at the three of us, who were still sniggering fit to burst.

"What are you laughing at?" she asked at last, disengaging her mouth from the plastic straw.

"Nothing," I managed to squeak before me and Chloe and Jen were off on one again.

Which, of course, I later realized, was exactly the *wrong* thing to say to my best friend.

Sandie had wangled coming back to mine again.

"Let's do our Physics homework together!" she'd suggested at afternoon break, like it was some big, exciting treat. But then, I was totally clueless when it came to Physics, so any help would be gratefully received. Only I hadn't quite figured out why we had to do the shared homework at my house and not hers.

I also hadn't figured out why Sandie had managed to convince herself that Jen, Chloe and I had been laughing at her when she came up to us in the morning. OK, so it explained why she'd looked so worried, but I still hadn't a clue why she thought her mates would do something like that to her. "Well, I knew *you* wouldn't be laughing at me," she'd replied after I'd explained that my Windowsill Bird Table was the butt of the joke, not her. "But sometimes I wonder about Chloe and Jen and the others…"

Why'd she think that? I'd wondered, but kept my mouth shut. Mainly because we were in our next class and our teacher had started talking…

Anyway, by the time the four o'clock bell went, I'd forgotten about all of that. It was time to escape from school and, after an hour spent trapped in the stuffiest classroom in the cosmiverse, I couldn't wait to get out of the door.

Only it didn't happen that quickly.

"Meet you outside!" Sandie whispered to me, as our dreaded Year Head, Mrs Fisher (boo, hiss), caught me in the corridor and decided to quiz me about my disappearing tie. (*Honestly*… I'd whipped it off as soon as I came out of that last class. Two minutes later I'd have been out of the school gates and out of her jurisdiction. How petty was the silly moo?)

I hated getting into trouble. I'd only taken off my rotten tie because it was so stupidly hot in Mr Samuels's class and he wouldn't open the windows 'cause of traffic noise (even though we were all dropping with heat exhaustion – well, nearly). So I let Mrs Fisher rant at me about not being out of school uniform on school property, while I wished (not for the first time) that I went to Highgate Wood School or one of the other schools in the area where you didn't have to wear a poxy uniform.

But, finally, Mrs Fisher's nagging was over. Finally, I got to escape outside, where I knew Sandie would be waiting for me, ready to hear me moaning about the unfairness of it all.

I pushed open the heavy main door, and there she was, over by the gate, talking to the usual gang of Chloe, Jen, Salma and Kellie. As I plodded down the steps, the other girls waved at me and headed off together, walking along the pavement in the direction of Crouch End Broadway.

"What was the less-than-lovely Mrs Fisher saying, then?" Sandie grinned at me as I drew level with her.

"Blah blah blah letting the school down; blah blah blah no respect; blah blah blah better improve my attitude," I joked, rolling my eyes.

Except that I didn't feel too much like joking, I was so mad and hurt at the injustice and pettiness of it all.

"Never mind her; she's just a rotten old witch," Sandie said comfortingly, slipping her arm into mine as we crossed the road.

I felt a little bit better. That's what best mates are for, isn't it? To tell you that crabby teachers are old witches. I squeezed Sandie arm and gave her a smile.

"You're right," I nodded, as we stepped on to the opposite pavement.

Now that we were out of harm's way (i.e. we'd crossed the road and didn't have to concentrate on avoiding rampaging buses and cars), I glanced back over my shoulder and looked at the distant figures of our other mates. "So where're Chloe and the others off to?"

"Kentucky Fried Chicken," Sandie answered.

Instantly, I felt taken aback. Since when did the other girls go to Kentucky Fried Chicken without asking us if we wanted to go?

"Well, thanks very much for the invite!" I grumbled, staring at my faraway friends while a bubble of hurt inflated in my chest.

First Mrs Fisher pounces on me and makes me feel like an axe murderer or something, and now my so-called mates were freezing me – and Sandie – out...

But it wasn't quite like that.

"Oh, they invited us," said Sandie, matter-of-factly.

"Huh?"

"But I said we didn't fancy it."

Excuse me? When had I said I didn't fancy it? When I was busy getting my head blasted off for the crime of being tie-less? After going through that, I might have liked to do something fun, like hanging out with my friends, *actually*…

Course, I didn't say any of that (I'm only good at arguing in my *head*). Instead, I came out with just the one word.

"Why?" I asked Sandie, baffled.

"Well, I thought it would be much nicer, just the two of us," she smiled, squeezing my arm again. "And anyway, I felt weird about Chloe and Jen, after the way they were laughing at me this morning."

"But I already told you," I protested, "they *weren't* laughing at you. None of us were!"

"Whatever," Sandie shrugged, sounding unconvinced. "Anyway, come on – let's get some nachos from the shop and take them back to yours!"

Whoopee. Nachos and Physics homework. Somehow it didn't quite compare with hanging out with the other girls and having a laugh.

Was it my imagination or was Sandie going a) totally paranoid, and b) clingy on me?

Chapter 7

TONIGHT, MATTHEW, I WILL BE...

"Look!" Kyra grinned, holding a really horrible, swirly-patterned polyester dress up against herself with one hand.

In the other, she was gripping a faded tartan shopping trolley, and on her head was a pink nylon marshmallow that was some kind of *hat*.

"And what are you supposed to be?" I asked her.

It was Wednesday and we'd just heard officially at school that Mr Bashir had approved the idea of Fancy Dress Friday next week. So, Sandie and me had decided to hit the charity shops after school and see if we could get our hands on some kind of outfit. And Kyra had invited herself along.

"An old lady with really bad taste!" Kyra said a little bit too loudly. "All I need to finish it off are those terrible woolly ankle-boots with the zips up the front! Bung them over, Ally!"

I smiled, but didn't reach for the boots – I was too aware of the dirty looks a lot of old ladies in the shop were chucking our way...

"What about this?" I heard Sandie say.

Me and Kyra both spun around and saw Sandie wearing a pair of seriously unflattering big specs on her nose and a dreary tweed jacket. She had this scrunched-up expression on her face as if she could smell poo at very close quarters.

"Mrs Fisher!" me and Kyra both exploded at once, instantly recognizing Sandie's impression of our deeply obnoxious (and deeply unfashionable) Year Witch. I mean, Year *Head*.

We were all giggling now, and getting more dirty looks from the not-so-young customers *and* the woman behind the counter. But I couldn't stop myself, and it was kind of nice to be having a laugh after feeling, well, *irritated* for most of today. Irritated with Sandie, that is...

I know I sound mean, but you'll understand in a minute. Picture the scene: it's five to nine this morning, and I'm hovering about in the corridor with Salma and Kellie before we have to trudge into French. None of my other friends have shown up yet. Then along comes Sandie, all smiley and pleased with herself. So I say, "What's up with you?" – dying to hear about whatever's got her looking so chuffed. "Look!" she says when she gets up close to us, and does this little twirl. It's her hair – in her hair she's got all these little plaits, same as mine. "I liked yours so much I decided to do it too! It took me ages, and it was really hard – I had to use two mirrors!"

I didn't care how hard it was or how many mirrors she'd used; all I could think of right then was what a pair of plonkers we'd look, sitting together through all our classes with this identical hairdo. And I wasn't being over the top – already I spotted Salma and Kellie giving each other a little look, and they were our *friends*. I couldn't stand thinking about the looks and sniggers we'd get off some of the other people in our class.

And they did giggle, though Sandie didn't seem to notice. So at breaktime, I went straight to the loo and took all my plaits out.

Big mistake.

My normal hair was its usual floppy, straight-ish self, but the ex-plaits were just a whole lot of crinkly frizz. I looked like a freak – like I was wearing two separate hairstyles at once. So I panicked, and stuck my head under the tap to flatten it all out. Then I tried to dry my hair under the hand-dryer, only people kept wanting to use it (how selfish! Couldn't they have just dried their hands on their blazers?), and when I *did* get a turn to use it, it kept cutting out – and then the bell went and I had to go back to class with a half-wet, half-dry, half-straight, half-frizzy hairdo. And that's when the sniggering *really* started.

"Why did you take your plaits out?" Sandie whispered to me, wide-eyed, as the teacher passed back our marked homework.

"Some of them were coming loose anyway," I lied.

It was funny, but no matter how grouchy I felt with her for copying me, I couldn't say it to her face – just like I couldn't bring myself to have a go at her about moving her knickers and pyjamas into my chest of drawers, *or* point out her clinginess. It's just that she's my best friend, and she's normally so sweet and nice... How could I start narking at her? We might have a fight or she might cry and I couldn't *bear* that.

At lunchtime, I went home, sorted my hair out and felt much better. And then, with the announcement about Fancy Dress Friday going ahead, all my irritation with Sandie faded away. Until this afternoon, when I saw her pull a little face as soon as Kyra asked to come along with us on our trawl through the charity shops. *There* was that clinginess rearing its head again, like she just wanted it to be me and her and no-one else... It was doing my head in.

So, anyway, that's why it was so nice to be having a laugh with Kyra and Sandie now – just seeing that my best mate had got her sense of humour back and was acting normal (as normal as you can when you're dressed up as Mrs Fisher) was a real relief.

It wasn't the shop assistant or an irate customer that finally burst the bubble on our giggle-fit. It was Kyra's mobile phone ringing.

"Urgh," Kyra groaned, searching in her bag for her phone. "I hope it's not Ricardo again. He keeps leaving messages for me. Why doesn't *he* get the message that I'm not going to answer them?"

Gulp.

I'd been so busy thinking about other stuff the last couple of days that I'd forgotten about Richie/Ricardo. But what if this was him phoning Kyra now? I felt swamped with guilt.

But how come? I asked myself. It wasn't as if I had anything to feel guilty about. I hadn't done anything with Richie/Ricardo. And I still hadn't a clue what he wanted, since Billy hadn't phoned me back with any information.

And – I tried to reason with myself – if he'd been pestering Kyra's answering service, that must mean he definitely *did* want to get back with Kyra (and definitely *wasn't* thinking about asking me out). So I should be glad *that* mystery was solved. Hopefully.

I guess ... well, I guess I just felt guilty because

I hadn't mentioned any of it to Kyra. Still, I didn't feel too fantastically comfortable at the idea of Kyra standing talking to her ex when I was hovering so close by. It was just too *weird*.

"Uh-oh," murmured Kyra, checking the number flashing on the phone's display. "It's my mum..."

And ... *relax*.

My shoulders sagged down with relief. It was only a parent, not an ex-boyfriend who'd secretly been trying to involve his girlfriend's mates in who-knows-what kind of complicated plot or plan.

I didn't relax for long, though, when I saw Kyra's face.

She was frowning like crazy, and although she was only saying stuff like "yes", "no" and "but" out loud, she was definitely mouthing swear-words at the receiver in between those "yes"s, "no"s and "but"s.

"OK. I said, OK!" she practically yelped, raising her voice and getting all the customers and staff staring dubiously at us for the zillionth time since we'd arrived.

"What's wrong?" I asked, as Kyra flipped her phone closed.

"My *mother* is what's wrong," she mumbled, shoving the naff dress back on to the clothes rack and dumping the pink marshmallow hat back on the shelf. "Sorry – I've got to go..."

And with that she was off, remembering only at the last minute that she was still holding on to the tartan trolley. She left it marooned in the middle of the shop floor as she flew out of the door.

"Wow, I wonder what's up with her mum this time?" I said to Sandie.

We knew Kyra's mother had some kind of problem to do with drinking, but Kyra had never told me or Sandie any more than that.

"Poor Kyra!" Sandie sighed. "I know how she feels…"

I took a sideways look at Sandie and wondered what that comment was supposed to mean. It was a pretty dumb thing to say, after all. Sandie maybe got a bit fed-up with how boring and over-protective her parents were, but that hardly compared to having an alcoholic in the house, did it?

Suddenly, I wasn't in the mood to carry on shopping – it didn't seem fun any more.

"Listen, I think I'll get off home too. I'll see you tomorrow, yeah?" I said as fast as I could, before Sandie could invite herself back to mine for the seventieth time that week…

Of course, all the way home, I felt guilty as anything for being so wound-up at Sandie.

What kind of best friend was I? A not very nice one, I decided gloomily.

Chapter 8

BIRD-BRAINED...

"Anyone want more bolognese?" asked Grandma, standing up and getting ready to grab the big bowl from the middle of the table.

Everyone shook their heads. Grandma had made *mounds* this Thursday night, and everyone was stuffed.

"But don't throw it away, Grandma!" Linn said urgently, making our gran pause beside the bin, and a patiently waiting Rolf.

"Why not?" she asked, staring at Linn through her thin, gold-framed glasses.

Rolf whined quietly, straining his nose towards the food that was so close and yet so far away...

"You could put some in a Tupperware box – for Ally to give to Sandie!" Linn continued drily. "I mean, Sandie hasn't been here for tea for the last two nights, so she must be missing it!"

"Ha, ha," I sneered at my big sister.

Urgh. My family now regularly seemed to be making digs about Sandie's presence in our house, which meant it had to be bad. Actually, I'd decided that maybe *that* was the problem recently; maybe Sandie wasn't being unusually clingy – maybe we were just seeing too much of each other. I really didn't want to get all ratty with my best friend, so I'd already decided that I should try and wangle it so we had a little bit of space from each other – and for a start that meant avoiding having her round for tea so often this week.

"How big is it?" asked Tor.

Good. I was glad of the distraction of Tor. Even if I couldn't remember what we'd been talking about.

"How big's what?" I asked, staring down into his plaintive brown eyes.

"The thing."

Ah, the thing. *Now* I remembered.

"About that big," I replied, picking a bit of spaghetti off my plate and holding it up in the air.

"What size of bird is it for?"

"All sizes of birds," I mumbled, stuffing my demonstration spaghetti in my mouth. "But the point is, it's for all kinds of people, living in all kinds of houses. The thing about it is that not everyone has a garden, but everyone's got a windowsill!"

It was Thursday teatime, and I was giving my family an update on my fantastic invention.

"So, the Windowsill Bird Table – is it going to make your fortune, then? Can we expect to see lots of them for sale up at Ally Pally garden centre soon?" Dad grinned at me, dimples appearing on his stubbly cheeks.

"Don't know about that," I smiled back.

Fat chance. It was already looking dicey that I'd get this first prototype in any fit state to be put into the craft fair, and it only consisted of about six bits of wood. I felt a bit dizzy at the very thought of making more than one…

"Well, I'm really looking forward to seeing it," said Grandma supportively. "In fact, I'm looking forward to seeing everyone's work."

"Are you going to come to the craft fair, Grandma?" I asked her.

That was the latest thing the teachers were drumming into us at school: telling us to let people know about the blimmin' fair. There wasn't much point in us making stuff if no one was going to come along and buy it…

"Yes, of course," said Grandma, nodding regally as if she were the Queen, coming along to preside over it ("I now declare this craft fair – in honour of the nice little girl with the scary bone disease that no one can pronounce – officially open!").

"Is Stanley going to go along to the fair with you,

Grandma?" Linn asked breezily, the hint of a smirk at her lips.

"Oh, he might and he might not. I haven't asked him yet," Grandma tried to say casually, but there was a definite pink flush to her cheeks.

Looked like she still felt a little shy in front of us all about the subject of lover-boy Stanley.

"And remember to pick up one of those posters from school tomorrow, one of you," Dad leapt in swiftly, pointedly glancing round the table at me, Rowan and Linn before any teasing of Grandma could escalate. "I'll put it up in my shop, since I won't be able to come along myself."

"But it can't be for big ones," said a small voice suddenly.

Around the table, five confused faces turned to look at Tor, wondering what on earth he was on about now.

And of us all, he was staring back at me.

"What can't be for big ones *what*?" I said ungrammatically as I frowned at him.

"Look!"

Tor spun his nearly empty plate round to show me something.

I stared at a long piece of spaghetti that had been positioned so that it made a wobbly-looking circle-ish thing. Then, underneath, another bit of spaghetti had been cut up and placed so it looked like a very small capital-letter "T".

"Hmmm…" I muttered, pretending I was studying a fine piece of modern art. "It's got a lot of depth and energy … could win the next Turner Prize!"

"It's a pigeon!" Tor sighed, as if it was obvious to any one with half a brain. Which wasn't me. Naturally.

"What's a pigeon? That blobby circle?" asked Rowan, getting up off her seat for a better look at the spaghetti art. "Ooh! Actually, I can see it now! Very good, Tor!"

"And *that* bit," Tor continued, pointing to the tiny T-shape, "is the Windowsill Bird Table!"

"Oh," I nodded, none the wiser and knowing that, *somewhere* along the line, Tor was trying to make a point.

"See?" he said, pointing from the "pigeon" to the T.

"Um, no," I gave in.

"Too big!"

"Ah! I get it!" Dad announced.

Oh, good. I'm glad somebody did. Maybe he could explain it to *me*.

"The bird table's going to be too small to hold the weight of big birds like pigeons!" said Dad, filling in the blanks.

"They could all fall over – and get hurt, like I did!" Tor exclaimed, pointing to the place on his forehead where the reddened bump had been.

"Wow – you know what this means, don't you, Ally?" said Linn, all mock-serious on the other side of the table from me.

"What?"

"You're going to have to paint a little sign on your bird table," she explained, narrowing her green eyes at me. "It'll have to say, 'Weight limit: three sparrows only'!"

"Yeah!" giggled Rowan. "With another sign underneath that says 'The management will not accept liability for any damage caused to fat pigeons who land here'!"

My sisters were off. Dad was choking over a mouthful of spaghetti. Even Grandma was chuckling. Only Tor was straight-faced, put out that no one was taking bird-safety seriously.

Out in the hallway, the front doorbell jangled.

"Brilliant – that'll be Billy," I said, scraping my chair on the floor as I escaped from the table and the teasing.

"Or maybe it's the Bird Health and Safety Officer from the council, come to check the premises for dangerously small bird tables!" I heard Linn call after me as I went to answer the front door.

"My room," I said to Billy, as soon as I'd yanked the door open and ushered my friend inside.

"Well, I'll just go and say hello first—"

"No you won't," I told him, steering him away from the kitchen and pushing him up the stairs. "They're being too silly tonight."

"Why?"

"Because they're my family and that's what they do," I shrugged, following him up the stairs.

"Hey, wait till I tell you about the fight that happened after school today!" Billy turned and grinned excitedly at me.

See? This was what I needed – lots of stupid gossip from Billy. I loved Sandie, but right now I was looking forward to talking rubbish with someone who wasn't paranoid, didn't leave half their wordly possessions in my house, and who would never *ever* dream of putting matching plaits in their hair.

But before Billy could start telling me about the fight after school (and give me any updates on the Richie/Ricardo situation), the phone began to ring.

"I'll get that – you go on up to my room," I told Billy, turning and pattering back down the stairs.

"Hello?" I said, expecting to hear the voices of one of my sisters' friends (and ever hopeful it might be Alfie calling for Linn – any excuse to talk to the most gorgeous being on the planet, even if

I never could think what to say to him beyond "Hold on; I'll go and get her!").

But the call wasn't for Linn or Rowan.

"Hi, Ally! It's just me."

Ooh, I hadn't heard that voice since ... we walked home together from school two hours ago.

"Hi, Sandie," I replied. "What's up?"

So much for having space from each other.

"Not much... I was just a bit bored and thought I'd phone to see what you were doing."

"Just had tea."

"Yeah? What did you have?"

"Bolognese."

"Yeah? I wish I'd come round to yours, then. Our tea was disgusting."

Hmm ... maybe Linn was right about the Tupperware box. I wondered if it wasn't too late to rescue the leftovers from the bin. Or Rolf.

"Listen, Sandie, can I call you back later?" I asked her. "It's just that Billy's here."

There was a tiny pause from the other end of the line, then I heard Sandie say, in this flat, almost accusing voice, "Oh. I didn't realize you were seeing him tonight."

What was up with her? Was I supposed to ask her permission first before I could invite Billy round? And I only met up with Billy once or twice a week, whereas I saw Sandie about a million times a day, so what was she so worried about? And another thing: I'd have happily seen the two of them together more often, if they just tried to get along together a bit better.

"Look, sorry, but I should get back to Billy," I repeated, knowing I sounded all apologetic but getting a little mad with myself for being that way. After all, Sandie was making me feel guilty for no reason.

"Fine! You just go and hang out with Billy!" said Sandie, in this quavering voice.

"Sandie?" I said questioningly.

"Bye!"

And that was it – she put down the phone on me.

Right, that's it, I decided. *If she's going to act like a sulky seven year old, I just can't be bothered.*

After all, I already had a seven year old to muck around with, and Tor wasn't even *sulky*.

I stomped back up the stairs, looking forward to a dumb conversation with my lovely, goofy, uncomplicated friend.

Chapter 9

ALL STEAMED UP

Sandie did it again.

OK, so she looked a bit sheepish when she slithered into her seat beside me in our first class the next day, but apart from that she acted like nothing had happened. And big cowardy-custard me did exactly the same.

Three classes later and we were in Design & Technology, with Sandie chattering away like there'd never been a blip between us, and me trying to get my stupid Windowsill Bird Table to stand without keeling over like the Leaning Tower of Pisa in a hurricane.

"...and Mum said, 'Come on! Eat up all your pudding!'" Sandie was telling me, "and you know something? I just couldn't help it; I just said, 'Leave me alone, Mum! Stop treating me like I'm a kid!'"

Hmm. Funny that I'd been thinking along those lines about Sandie only the night before...

"What did she say when you said that?" I asked, adjusting my super-sexy plastic goggles (if only

Alfie could see me in those ... he'd be just *wild* with lust!).

"She got all huffy and hurt and stomped off to the kitchen."

Sandie looked quite pleased with herself when she announced that. Which was weird. She maybe had a moan to me any time her folks fussed around her too much, but she was never horrible to them. I know lots of people argue and snap at their parents, but Sandie wasn't one of those people.

Well, not up until now.

"What did you do then?" I quizzed her, while eyeing up the very boring but very *straight* shelf she was making.

(Straight... I liked that. I wondered for a moment whether she'd let me buy it from her, so I could have something to enter in the craft fair that people wouldn't laugh at. Then I remembered that my entire class would know that it was Sandie's, so I'd be rumbled straight away. Rats...)

"I didn't do anything," shrugged Sandie, crossing her arms over her chest. "I just carried on watching TV. Anyway, she deserved it."

Now Mrs Walker ... she's not the sort of person that I'd want as a mum. She's just way too *mumsy* (in that spitting-on-a-tissue-and-wiping-your-face-in-public way), and she does twitter and fluster all the time. (Actually, if you've ever seen the film *Chicken Run*, think of Babs the dippy hen who clucks around knitting things and you'll get a good picture of Sandie's mum.)

But for all her clucking and worrying, Mrs Walker's still pretty nice. And whenever I see her do stuff like kiss and cuddle Sandie (which she does a *lot*), it does make me feel a bit funny inside, like I wish *my* mum was around to do that...

So when Sandie started slagging her off, I was stunned.

"*Why* does your mum deserve it?" I squinted at Sandie, through a slowly-building mist.

(While I was talking I was struggling so hard to get a wonky nail out of my bird table that my goggles were steaming up. Maybe I should have thought about inventing Windscreen Wipers for Goggles instead of the rotten Windowsill Bird Table.)

"Ally, you don't know what she's been like lately," said Sandie, an invisible black cloud passing over her face. "Her *and* dad."

"What do you—?"

The last word of that sentence was "mean", but I didn't get it out. Sandie interrupted me, her face suddenly lighting up.

"Oh, I meant to tell you – I'm going to paint my room this weekend. I'm sick of that baby pink. Do you want to come and help me?"

OK – I got the hint: she didn't want to sound off any more about her mum and dad in class in case anyone overheard. (She wasn't the only one – Kyra had been very quiet about the phone call she'd had from her mum the day before, when she'd bolted out of the charity shop.)

"Course I'll come and help you paint! That'll be fun!" I assured her.

Actually, I was pretty pleased by the news. Sandie's room was long, long, *long* overdue for redecoration; the only reason she'd never done it before was because her mum and dad thought the wall-to-wall Barbie pink was too cute for words. (Too *revolting* for words, more like.)

I was also pleased because after a week of being a bit clingy and moody, this sounded like Sandie had decided to do something positive. So of course I was going grab a paintbrush and help.

"I was thinking of doing it on Sunday – if you help me and we start early, we could easily get it done in a day. Is that OK for you?" Sandie blinked questioningly at me.

Let's see … lunch with Prince William; shopping trip with Britney Spears in New York; pampering day at an exclusive health spa with Kylie Minogue…

Nope, I wasn't doing any of those, so it looked

like I'd be free on Sunday. Except, of course, for one little snag. A little snag in a baseball cap.

"No problem," I shrugged at her. "I'll have to blow Billy out, but he won't mind."

Even through my steamed-up goggles, I saw Sandie smile herself a little secret smile as soon as I said that...

Chapter 10

RICHIE/RICARDO REVEALS ALL...

"Don't do that, Tor," I said, pushing the feather wand away from my nose.

It was Saturday morning and me and my brother were ambling back home after our regular weekly stock-up at the pet shop. Once we'd grabbed all the necessities, like fish food and hamster bedding, Tor had somehow managed to steer my attention towards the *non*-necessities, and I'd ended up forking out £1.99 for a black plastic stick with luminous pink feathers stuck on the end.

Apparently – according to Tor – the wand thing he was now wiggling in my face was the cats' favourite toy, but their last one went mysteriously missing several weeks before. Actually, when he'd said that, I suddenly realized that I knew what had happened to it. One night I'd woken up to the sound of crunching coming from under my bed, and when I'd investigated, I found Winslet was staring back at me with a mangled length of plastic in her jaws and a flurry of luminous pink feathers stuck to her nose and paws. I hadn't a clue what it was at the time; I was just glad she hadn't eaten any of my trainers for a while, so I went back to sleep.

"Hee, hee!" giggled Tor, lobbing the feathery end of the wand into my ear this time.

"Tor, that's *kind* of annoying," I said, yanking the thing out of his hand as we walked.

"*Rolf* likes it when I do that," Tor huffed.

"Yeah, but Rolf's dumb."

"No he's not!" said Tor defensively.

"Yes, he is!" I laughed. "Rolf's so dumb he tries to eat *bees*!"

It was true. Every summer it was the same: Rolf would be out in the garden, spot himself a bee, snap at it as if it was a tasty flying dog-treat and then end up at the vet's with a badly stung tongue. He never learnt.

"How's Freddie?" I asked, trying to distract Tor from the subject of the cat toy by chatting about one of his favourite school friends.

"Horrible."

"Horrible how? Is he *feeling* horrible, or do you *think* he's horrible?"

"I *think* he's horrible."

"Why?"

"He says Charmaine's his best friend now," Tor shrugged.

Tor and Freddie seem to fall out with each other regularly – and then, just as regularly, be best buddies again.

Now, I know that two boys having typical seven-year-old spats was a world away from me and Sandie, but what he'd just said really made me think. Something in our rock-solid friendship was going slightly wobbly and I couldn't quite put my finger on what it was. But part of it definitely was to do with some kind of jealousy Sandie felt about me and Billy.

The last thing I wanted to do was hassle her about it, but I decided that, since we'd be alone together next day, painting her room, I'd *definitely* take the opportunity to talk to her about it.

If the subject came up.

Maybe.

Oh, why couldn't she just go back to normal so I didn't have to feel uncomfortable like this?

Tor and I had by now reached home, where Rolf and Winslet set up a welcoming howling-and-barking committee as I struggled to find the front-door keys with my hands full of plastic bags and wands.

Just as my fingers clamped around the cold metal of the keys, the door was opened from the inside and a jumble of paws and general hairiness came tumbling out.

Rowan stood yawning on the doormat, dressed – or, more accurately, *not* dressed – in her white cotton, Victorian-style nightie.

"Give us a couple of those," said Rowan, holding out her hands to grab some pet-shop bags from me and Tor. "Ooh, *that's* nice!"

I realized what she was gazing at: it was the luminous feathery wand, which I was unconsciously wafting in the air like some dorky fairy princess. I might have guessed that Rowan would like it.

"You're up early!" I commented, following her inside and passing the wand over to Tor.

At the weekends, Rowan doesn't "do" mornings. While the rest of us are all up and about, yelling at each other over the sound of radios and TVs and scampering dogs, Rowan sleeps blissfully on, dreaming dreams of spangly things. Probably.

"Got woken by the phone," she yawned again, padding barefoot ahead of us along the hall, towards the kitchen and the utility room, where all the pet munchies, etc. were kept.

"Yeah? Who was it?" I asked, looking forward to dumping the heavy bags that were by now gently cutting off the blood supply to my fingers.

"Some lad, for you."

I froze, with one foot hovering just above the floor. Not expecting me to stop suddenly like that,

Tor stumbled into the back of me and jolted me forward.

"Are you OK?" asked Rowan, turning round at the racket of "Oomphs!" and thumps and rustling bags going on behind her.

"Yes, sure," I nodded, trying to stand up straight and regain my composure. "Um, who was it?"

"Some lad called ... hold on – I wrote it down," said Rowan, dropping the bags she was carrying on to the kitchen floor and picking up a torn bit of paper from the table.

"Well?" I squeaked, unable to handle the suspense.

"Um, I think he said his name was Ricky," Rowan frowned down at her own handwriting.

"You mean Richie?"

Omigod. He had called. I didn't think he'd ever actually do it.

"Richie ... yes, it could have been Richie," Rowan nodded. "Anyway, he said can you meet him today, up at the skating rink at Ally Pally, at two o'clock."

Right at that moment, I was really glad that Rowan was a) not naturally nosey, and b) still half-asleep. Mainly because it meant she wasn't going to give me a hard time about why my face had just gone as luminous pink as the feathery bits on the new cat toy...

*M*M*

OK, here was my dilemma…

If Richie/Ricardo wanted to talk to me about Kyra, why hadn't he just left his number, and asked for me to call him back? If he wanted to ask me about his chances with my friend, then all that could be spoken about over the phone – right?

But now he'd asked to meet me in person. Almost like a … a date. Aaarrgghh – what if that stupid suspicion of mine had been right after all? What if he was planning to ask me out? What would he say? What would *I* say? Why was I back to feeling worried and sick and sort of excited again?

When it came down to it, I was far too nervous to face him on my own. I needed back-up. I needed what Grandma would have called a "chaperone". So…

"Can I have an ice-cream?"

"Absolutely," I nodded, as Tor and I walked into the vast entrance-cum-café at the Alexandra Palace skating rink.

I couldn't see Richie/Ricardo, but that could have been down to sheer panic-blindness, I knew.

"Are you coming skating too?" Tor looked up at me dubiously.

Was he kidding? I couldn't walk in shoes with *heels*, never mind boots with slivers of metal holding them up.

"No – I'll just watch you. While I talk to my … um … friend."

"Is your friend here yet?"

"I don't think so."

"Can I have some money?"

"What for?"

"Boots?"

"Oh, uh, of course," I bumbled, rummaging in my pocket for coins to pay the boot-hire fee.

And so I found myself watching Tor swirl over the ice, frozen to my plastic seat with cold and utter fear.

Tor was oblivious; while I waited for my "friend", he'd already run (skated, more like) into his own little friend, someone called Daniel who was in his class at school.

"Hi, uh, Ally," I heard Richie/Ricardo mumble.

Wow – I didn't even know he knew my name. Usually, he'd just call me "Hey, you" or "Hey, you; Kyra's mate".

Actually, him calling me Ally felt a bit too intimate for my liking.

"Thanks for, ahem, coming," he coughed nervously.

"That's OK," I mumbled, plucking up the courage to look at him.

Looks-wise, I understood why Kyra might have

fallen for Richie/Ricardo. Before I'd ever met him, she'd told me he could be in a boy band, he was so cute. (Actually, strictly speaking, there're quite a lot of uglies in boys bands; and usually only a couple of cute ones up front. Take a closer look next time one of them is on *Top of the Pops* and see what I mean: it's definitely a 3:2 ugly/cute ratio.)

Just as I was staring at Richie/Ricardo's undeniably handsome face, there was a dull *thunk*! as Tor came to a speedy stop against the rink wall beside us. Panting, he leant his elbows on the railing and stared hard at my "friend".

"Oi! Bog off, kid!" Richie/Ricardo snarled in my brother's direction.

Ah ... *now* I remembered why I'd never liked this guy much. Cute on the outside does not necessarily mean cute on the inside.

"This is my brother," I told him drily, my nervousness disappearing now that I remembered I was dealing with a rude git.

"Oh ... right. Whatever," Richie/Ricardo shrugged.

Tor narrowed his eyes at him and gave a full-on, silent stare. It was the sort of stare that regularly freaks Billy out and makes him refer to Tor as Spook-kid. It looked like it was freaking Richie/Ricardo out too.

"Do ... do you want to go and get a Coke or

something?" he asked me, pointing in the direction of the café.

I was so cold I could do with drinking a vat of tea to warm up, but I wasn't going to shift just because Richie/Ricardo wanted me to.

"No, I'm fine here," I replied, trying to stop my teeth from chattering. "I've got to keep an eye on Tor."

"*Tor!*" Richie/Ricardo repeated, scoffing at my brother's name.

OK, so it's unusual, but no one scoffs at my brother's name and *lives*. Boy, I was getting to like this guy less and less by the second.

"Yes, his name's *Tor*. Now, what did you want to see me about?" I said sternly, while Tor gazed on at us both.

Then the strangest thing happened to Richie/Ricardo: his conceited face crumpled to the point that I thought he might actually *blub*.

"She won't listen to me," he mumbled, dropping his head down and speaking to his shoes.

"Kyra?" I prompted him.

He nodded.

"I really ... I really want her back, Ally, but she won't answer my calls!"

I knew. I'd been there when she'd said so.

"You're her best mate," he continued mumbling.

Was I? Thinking about it, I supposed I *was* her closest friend in Crouch End, even though there was still lots I didn't know about her.

"And 'cause you're her best mate, I need you to do me a favour..."

"What?" I frowned at the top of his head, since he was still staring at the concrete floor.

"I need you to take this," he said, pulling a cassette out of his jacket pocket and handing it to me, "round to her house."

"Um, well, that could be a bit of a problem," I told him, staring at the blank tape he'd just handed me. "I've never been to her house. I mean, I know what street she lives in, but I don't know the number or anything."

"I do. Well, I haven't been round there either, but I know her address," he said, rooting around in his jacket pocket and then coming back out with a piece of scribbled-on paper.

"Why don't you post this, if you have her address?" I quizzed him, wondering what on earth was on the tape.

"'Cause if she sees my handwriting, she might just chuck it away."

Taking the piece of paper from him, I exchanged glances with Tor, who seemed to find this all very fascinating.

"Y'see, if you go round to her house this afternoon ... well, she'll listen to you," he bumbled, "and you can make her listen to my tape!"

"Can I?" I wondered out loud.

Kyra seemed pretty strong-willed to me. I couldn't see her ever letting me persuade her to do anything she didn't want to.

"Please help me, Ally..."

He was still gazing at his feet. I looked from his head to Tor, trying to fathom out what I should do.

Tor was now staring at Richie/Ricardo with the sort of sympathetic gaze he usually saves for sickly animals. Still, Richie/Ricardo was a bit of a pig, so maybe it was fair enough.

"You should help him," Tor nodded at me seriously.

"Aw, thanks, Ally!" Richie/Ricardo suddenly exclaimed, lifting his head and giving me a grateful grin, even though I hadn't agreed to do anything yet. "Come on, you can go now! She'll probably be in! She doesn't do much on Saturday afternoons!"

"But I can't!" I fumbled. "I've got Tor!"

"I can play with Daniel! And his mum will drive me home after!" Tor announced.

Wow – between them, these two boys had decided everything for me. And so, after a quick conversation with Daniel's mum, I found myself stomping off down the hill in the direction of Kyra Davies's house, with a mysterious tape in my hand and a nervous, twisty knot of excitement in my stomach.

Chapter 11

SING-A-LONG-A-ROBBIE

OK, so curiosity had a lot to do with it.

Doing this good deed for Richie/Ricardo was the perfect excuse for me to be shallow and find out more about Kyra, her house and her life, basically.

And part of her life was staring at me right now.

"Um, hello. Is ... is this where Kyra lives?" I blabbered.

Because you surely can't be Kyra's alcoholic horror of a mother, I thought to myself, looking at this petite, smiling, very together-looking woman.

"Yes, it is," the woman surprised me by replying. "Although she's out right now. And you are...?"

"I'm Ally. I'm her friend. From school," I said.

Come to be nosey, I *didn't* say.

The woman wasn't much like Kyra; she was a lot smaller, a lot curvier and the only thing giving her skin colour was a coat of perfectly applied make-up.

"Ally? I haven't heard of you. But then Kyra never tells me anything," she laughed, rolling her eyes. "Was she expecting you, Ally?"

About as much as I was expecting you to be this nice…

"Um, no," I shrugged, letting my eyes quickly dart over Mrs Davies's Gap clothes. "I was just passing and … uh … wanted to give her a tape I'd promised her."

Automatically, my eyelid started twitching. Served me right for lying through every gap in my teeth…

"Well, come on in – she's out with her dad, but they should be back any minute."

So there I was, sitting in Kyra's fancy modern kitchen (which made mine at home look like a *shack*), having coffee and a chat with her very charming, very friendly mum, when Kyra and her dad arrived home.

"Ally!" she exclaimed, standing totally startled in the kitchen doorway.

"Hi!" I tried to grin, feeling like I was as welcome as a burglar or *rabies* or something, the way she was looking at me.

Which was a bit much, really, when you think of how Kyra behaved when she first started at our school a couple of months ago. She really freaked me out, then, turning up at my house unannounced all the time. And that wasn't the half of it; back then I couldn't stand the way she was such a drama queen, always showing off all the time. I remember that I even thought she might be a bit of a liar...

And right now, that last thought was sneakily wriggling into my brain again. After all, Mrs Davies didn't come across as some demanding, crazy drunk, like Kyra had made out. In the ten minutes we'd been alone together, Kyra's mum had been polite and friendly; not shouty and scary. She didn't slur when she asked me questions about school and about how Kyra was getting on. She was sipping on tea, not knocking back vodka.

Kyra was so weird about having anyone back to her house; was this perhaps the reason? That she'd made up the whole thing about her mum being an alcoholic when she first knew me and Sandie, and she was too embarrassed to tell us it was all a big balloon-sized fib?

"Ben, this is Kyra's friend Ally," Mrs Davies smiled at the tall man standing behind Kyra. "Ally, this is Kyra's dad. I just thought I'd introduce you, since Kyra's too rude to do it!"

"Hi there, Ally!" he beamed, looking genuinely pleased to see me, which was more than Kyra did.

I could see who she took after now – Kyra definitely had her dad's height and skinnyness, as well as a paler, honey version of his dark skin.

"Let's go to up to my room," Kyra suddenly

announced, finding her voice at last and fixing me with a come-now-and-no-arguing glare.

"OK," I nodded, slipping off my stool and following her out of the kitchen. "Thanks for the coffee, Mrs Davies!"

"Pleasure," Kyra's mum smiled after me as she cleared the cups away and began chatting to her husband.

I stared at Kyra's back and wondered what she was thinking.

"Nice house!" I said conversationally, as she stomped up the stairs with me trailing behind her.

What else could I say? "Hey, Kyra, by the way – all that stuff about your mum's drinking problems, was that just lies?"

Um … *no*. I somehow didn't suppose I *could* come out with that. And expect to live.

"You think this is nice? You should have seen our last place in Rye," Kyra replied over her shoulder, thankfully unable to psychically tune into my thoughts at that precise moment. "It was this totally huge old house; we got it dead cheap, and Dad fixed it every spare minute he got. We sold it for a fortune when we had to leave!"

Had to leave.

What was it Kyra had once told us? That she'd had to start at loads of new schools over the years, because every time her family settled somewhere her mum would end up doing something to embarrass them through her drinking… Yeah, and then her dad would apply for *another* transfer with the bank he worked for, and they'd be on the move *again*.

But was any of that true?

"And this is my room," said Kyra, ushering me into a huge, bright bedroom full of trendy, IKEA-ish furniture. "I haven't got any pictures or anything up on the walls yet – I've got to get rid of that naff wallpaper first…"

I could see what she meant – the floral paper didn't go with either the furniture *or* with Kyra.

"Yeah? That's funny – I'm going round to Sandie's tomorrow to help her do up *her* room," I chattered away, trying to sound normal, even if I didn't feel it.

Kyra closed the bedroom door, then sank down against it with her back, her eyes closed.

"Are you OK?" I frowned at her, my heart leap-frogging about in my chest.

"Yeah … just relieved that she's on her best behaviour today."

"She" was obviously Mrs Davies. And "best behaviour" obviously meant she was sober. I bit my lip and tried to read Kyra's face, to see if I could figure out whether she was telling the truth or spinning me a line.

"Your mum seems ... nice," I said feebly.

"Oh, yeah, she can be dead nice," Kyra sighed, fixing me with a meaningful stare and strolling over to the bed, where she sat herself down, curling her long skinny legs under her. "But catch her on the wrong day, and it's like sodding Jekyll and Hyde round here."

She *looked* like she was telling the truth. She *sounded* like she was telling the truth...

"Anyway, how come you're here?" she blinked at me.

Can you believe it? I'd forgotten all about the tape that was stuffed in my pocket: the whole reason I was round at Kyra's in the first place.

"Well..." I began, pulling the tape out. "Remember my friend Billy?"

Kyra scrunched up her forehead and looked blank.

"Richie – I mean, Ricardo's mate. *My* friend Billy. The one you and Ricardo set me up with when we went to that party?"

Kyra started sniggering at the memory of that disastrous moment. I mean, how embarrassing was that? Going on a blind date and finding out it's your own best friend? Urgh ... don't remind me.

"Well, Billy said Ricardo wanted to meet me – to

talk about you," I added hastily. "And so I saw him just now, and he asked me to give you this…"

I walked over and joined her, perching on the edge of the bed and handing her the tape.

"A blank cassette?" Kyra frowned at it, flipping the plastic case back and forth in her hand.

"It's not blank. It's a compilation tape he's done for you – to show you how he feels about you…"

"Oh, puh-*lease*!" Kyra groaned, flopping back on the bed and tossing the tape to one side. "How many times do I have to tell him I don't want to go out with him any more?"

Kyra probably had a point, but out of some misguided sense of fairness to Richie/Ricardo, I felt she should give the tape a listen.

Glancing around the room, I saw an expensive-looking silver midi-system on top of a chest of drawers.

"Look, just five minutes, OK?" I suggested, bounding across the floor and fidgeting with the tape deck.

"Whatever…" sighed Kyra, still flopped back on the bed.

Scouring all the fancy buttons, I finally found the right one and pressed "play".

Out came Robbie Williams (well, not personally – he's a bit too big and muscly to fit inside a midi-system), singing "She's the One".

"Sorry, Ricardo – but I'm *not* the one," Kyra muttered above the music.

Looked like she wasn't too impressed.

"You know, I never got why people liked this track so much – it's so horribly slushy. I like fast, loud stuff; not stupid, soppy ballads. And if Ricardo liked me the way he says he does, he should know that," she ranted on. "I mean, if he'd put on something like Nirvana or –"

Kyra stopped, suddenly aware of what she was hearing. Slowly, she raised herself up on to her elbows and stared at me. I stared back, not quite believing my ears.

After only a couple of minutes, Robbie had been faded out ... to be replaced by someone – Richie/Ricardo, presumably – warbling away karaoke-style in his place.

And then he was drowned out ... by me and Kyra howling our heads off.

Poor Richie/Ricardo; how could we ever look at the big-headed plonker again and keep a straight face?

Chapter 12

ONE LUMP OR TWO?

Somewhere along the road on the way back from Kyra's (in-between frightening passing strangers by sniggering out loud at the memory of Richie/Ricardo's excruciatingly terrible singing), I had an Illuminating Thought.

Yep, I finally figured out *why* I'd had that funny, excited feeling when I thought Richie/Ricardo might ask me out... All it came down to was flattery.

Oh, yes, I'm that shallow.

The thought that someone might fancy me enough to ask me out had made me go stupidly giddy at the very idea. And it hadn't even mattered if that someone turned out to be Richie/Ricardo Esposito, someone I fancied not one tiny bit. (Not that it mattered; he fancied himself quite enough, especially when it came to singing.)

Pathetic, right? Still, at least I wasn't as pathetic as Richie/Ricardo...

I couldn't help grinning again at the memory of him warbling away on the tape. (And he did it loads of times too; there'd be some well-known, slushy love song, followed by Richie/Ricardo acting like he was auditioning for *Stars In Their Eyes* or something.)

"What are you laughing at?" asked Tor, surprising me by getting out of a car that had drawn up beside me just as I approached the house.

"Nothing!" I smiled at him, then noticed Daniel's mum beckoning me.

"I hope it's all right!" she said, looking at me apologetically. "The fish, I mean! Frankly, it's been giving me the shudders, and when Tor came back to our house to play after skating and said he'd take it, well..."

I hadn't a clue what she was going on about, till I saw Daniel pass out a wobbling, clear-plastic bag to Tor.

"Look!" said Tor, his face radiating happiness.

I looked.

And saw a goldfish with a very strange lump on its side.

So, it seemed as if we had a new addition to our animal hospital.

"No problem!" I nodded at Daniel's mum, and gave the car door a shove closed. "Come on, then, Tor – let's introduce him to the cats..."

And with that, Tor and I strolled up the path

and into the house, both smiling at the way our day had turned out.

Who'd have thought that a mysterious meeting with a twerp like Richie/Ricardo could have made me laugh more than I had done in ages, *and* led to the beginning of a beautiful friendship between my little brother and Lumpy the goldfish…?

Miffed.

That was the only word to describe Sandie's mood when I told her what I'd been up to.

When Tor and I walked back into the house, I found her in the living room, watching some ancient black and white movie on telly and sharing a packet of Hobnobs with Rowan.

"Why didn't you phone and let me know that he called you?" Sandie demanded, sounding bruised and hurt.

I looked over at Rowan, who shrugged, looking guilty for having obviously told Sandie about Richie/Ricardo's phone call earlier in the day.

"And you took *Tor* to the ice rink with you?" she blinked at me accusingly.

Uh-oh.

Course, that was nothing compared to how miffed she was when I told her I'd been hanging out at Kyra's all afternoon. She didn't even laugh when I told her about Richie/Ricardo and his pathetic *yodelling*. Rowan did, though, but soon stopped sniggering when Sandie shot her a look that said "traitor!".

"I'm sorry!" I found myself apologizing to Sandie. "I just got stressed out about him phoning, and … and I guess I never thought!"

You know, maybe that was true. But if I was suddenly to turn into Ricki Lake or Esther or someone (actually, make that Ricki Lake – she's not groovy, but she's a lot groovier than Esther), and actually analysed the situation, I'd probably tell myself (in an American accent, natch) that subconsciously I hadn't wanted to include Sandie in any of this exciting stuff – just in case she put a downer on it all.

Ooh, that sounded mean, but it was probably about right. Unfortunately.

"Um… Sandie came round to show you the paint she's bought to do up her bedroom," Rowan said cheerfully, as if she was trying to thaw out the frost that was hanging in the air between me and my so-called best friend.

"I phoned you earlier, to see if you wanted to come to Fads with me and help me choose," Sandie added, fixing me with a look that told me I'd let her down. "So I went on my *own*, and then

I came straight round here. I *assumed* you'd be back…"

Which I wasn't.

Wow, what a terrible person I was – if you were checking things out through Sandie's big blue eyes.

"Yeah?" I replied, summoning up a smile. "What colour *did* you get?"

"This one," said Sandie, brightening up a little as she pulled a heavy pot of paint out of a rustling Fads bag. "It's lovely, isn't it?"

Yes, it was lovely. "Blue Babe", it was called. I can safely say that I liked the lovely "Blue Babe" a lot. Mainly because it was the colour my *own* room was painted in.

You know something? The way things were going, I'd have to give my shadow the sack. I didn't need it any more; not with Sandie around, dogging my every step and copying my every move…

Chapter 13

MUTANT DAISIES

I love my room.

I love the cosy, sloping attic walls (even if I do sometimes bash my head on them when I'm half-asleep or just in a plain stupid state of mind). I love the view out of the window towards Alexandra Palace. I love all the books in my wooden book-shelf. I love my music system (even if the tape deck goes a bit wonky sometimes, speeding up and slowing down tapes when I least expect it). I love the blow-up globe that hangs from the ceiling and lets me daydream about all the places in the world I can travel to. I love my duvet cover that's covered in clouds. I love the map on the wall, where I stick pins to show all the places Mum's sent us cards and letters from. I love the fact that all the furrballs (of a catty and dogsome nature) come padding up here to snooze, just because it's so comfy. And I love the colour of the walls.

Which is *why* I didn't want to see the exact same blue on Sandie's walls.

This is daft! I thought to myself, pulling an ancient checked shirt of my dad's on over my T-shirt. *Coming over all possessive about a colour! But it would be the same if Sandie suddenly started dressing the same as me, or copied my hairdo. Oh, except she did that already, didn't she?*

"It's going to be so nice to get rid of all this pink, isn't it?" Sandie smiled at me, her white neck looking all skinny and swan-long where it stuck out of the collar of an old, paint-splattered sweatshirt that must have belonged to her father. Down below the sweatshirt, her legs looked equally skinny in a pair of ratty, outgrown black leggings.

"Ungh," I grunted, wafting my paintbrush over the pot of "Blue Babe".

What was particularly annoying me was the thought of the paint-colour chart that I'd found on the floor beside her bed when we'd been moving all the furniture to the centre of the room (out of splattering range). "Happy Violet", "Yellow Groove", "Tropical Lime", "Honey Bee", "Spicy Salsa" ... they all sounded and looked brilliant. Why couldn't Sandie have chosen one of *them* instead of *my* "Blue Babe"?

Still, I had a chance to make a suggestion (Rowan's, actually), that would at least make this whole room less of a carbon copy of mine. But if I *was* going to suggest it, I had to do it now, before it was too late…

"Do a paint effect!" Rowan had said eagerly the night before, once Sandie had left and I'd had a good old moan about the game of Paint Snap! my best friend seemed to want to play with me.

"What *kind* of paint effect?" I'd asked her dubiously, instantly imagining Laurence Llewelyn-Bowen projecting rude (and nude) Greek classical figurines on to the door in Sandie's room that hid the central-heating boiler.

"Well, what if you drew huge flowers on the walls? Just simple outlines of petals?" Rowan sighed happily, getting carried away with her idea. "Then you paint all the walls blue except for the petals, so you're left with big pink daisies all around the room!"

It sounded mental, but it was definitely a) better than it looking exactly like my room, and b) a vast improvement on the sugar-coated pink abomination Sandie had lived in for the past few years.

So I suggested it.

"Wow! Do you think we could? But how would we do it?!" trilled Sandie, obviously knocked sideways by the concept of mutant daisies staring down at her when she slept.

"Like this…" I answered quickly, pulling out a

small-scale sketch that my fabulous saviour of a sister Rowan had doodled for me the night before.

And so we did it, drew mammoth flowers on the walls in pencil then filled in most of the walls with swathes of liquid blue. While we worked, we chatted about fluffy, nothingy stuff, like the movie that was on TV the night before, and who the cutest dead bloke in the universe was (we ended up with a draw between River Phoenix and Kurt Cobain). We flicked the radio between Radio One and Capital, depending how much we hated the songs that were playing, and sang along loudly to the ones we loved. (Something we wouldn't have done if Sandie's parents had been at home. Singing out loud would definitely have got Mrs Walker in a twitter, in case we were disturbing the neighbours or the plants growing in the garden or something).

It was amazing; we'd been at it for only a couple of hours and already we were nearly finished. In fact, all that was left to do was for Sandie to tidy up the edges of the petals using a thinner brush, while I stuck my tongue in the corner of my mouth and carefully began to paint along the skirting board. (Note: sticking your tongue out of the corner of your mouth does NOT make your hand any steadier. Trust me: I know. And if you don't believe me, just take a close look in Sandie's room sometime.)

OK, so despite the fact that Sandie had hijacked "Blue Babe", we were getting on pretty well. Next on my agenda *had* to be to ask why she was acting so weird lately.

But ... um ... *first*, I decided – chicken that I was – I might just chat a bit about something else, till I worked up the courage to go into all that sensitive stuff...

"Oh, I meant to tell you," I began, still keeping my eye on the straight(ish) line I was trying to draw with my brush.

"What's that?" came Sandie's voice from the other side of the room.

"Well, you know how I was round at Kyra's yesterday?"

If the radio hadn't been playing, you could have heard a pin drop. The silence would have been so deafening that my words could have echo-echo-echoed round the room.

"Did you hear me, Sandie?" I glanced up and checked with her.

She looked engrossed in the big petal that was forming on the wall, but managed the faintest "Mmm".

"It just that when I was round there, I met her mum."

Normal Sandie would have responded to that

little nugget with something like, "Ooh, *really*? Well, what's she *like*?" Actually, *Normal* Sandie wouldn't have waited for me to bring the subject up; *Normal* Sandie would have asked me a million questions about every tiny corner of Kyra's house by now and every last shred of a detail about her parents – especially her mum.

But I wasn't dealing with Normal Sandie; I was dealing with her parallel-universe weird twin.

And all *Weird* Sandie had to say was, "Oh."

For a second, I was tempted to run across the room and shake her, demanding that the aliens who'd abducted my brilliant friend bring her back straight away. That, or consult the Yellow Pages for my nearest local witch and ask her to break the evil spell surrounding Sandie and let her be her nice, normal self again.

Instead, I just carried on with my painting, and with the conversation I was having. With myself. (For all the interest Sandie that was showing.)

"Anyway, Kyra's mum seemed really friendly and everything. I sat and talked to her for ages, till Kyra got home. She was asking me all the questions about school and was acting all interested, you know?"

Silence.

"And I just thought, 'Wow, *this* doesn't sound like the freak that's always drunk and giving Kyra grief!' And then it kind of hit me, do you think Kyra maybe – y'know – made that stuff up? It's just that—"

"Kyra, Kyra, *Kyra*! That's all you *ever* talk about!"

I froze to the spot. If I wasn't very much mistaken, that screechy, shouty voice belonged to Sandie. Only I had to look at her and make sure, since I'd never heard her speak like that in the two years we'd been best mates.

"Wha-what?" I blabbered in shock.

"It's all '*Kyra* said this' and '*Kyra* said that', and 'Is *Kyra* going to go out with Ricardo again?' and 'Me and *Kyra* had such a laugh yesterday'!"

"Sandie! That is *so* not true!" I blurted out.

I don't know what she'd been planning to say after that, because a ring at the doorbell stopped her in her tracks. With a huff of her shoulders, Sandie turned and left me in the room, wondering madly if I was still asleep in my own blue room and having some kind of blue-tinged nightmare.

And blue-tinged or not, this nightmare was just about to get more complicated.

I heard voices at the door, followed by a slam, and then two sets of footsteps coming towards Sandie's room.

"Hi! It's only me!" said Kyra, slouching casually into the room behind a tight-lipped Sandie.

"I remembered you said yesterday that you'd be round here painting today."

"Uh, yeah," I shrugged, noticing that Sandie had immediately picked up her brush and turned her attention back to the wall again.

"Jeez..." gasped Kyra, suddenly noticing our handiwork for the first time. "It's like being in *Honey, I Shrunk the Kids*!"

It was true – each flower was as big as one of us, if we were doing a star-jump.

To get the full effect, Kyra plonked herself down on the bed in the middle of the room and stared around.

"Are you going to give us a hand, then?" I grinned at her. "There's another paintbrush over there..."

"Nah," Kyra replied, wrinkling up her freckle-speckled nose. "Don't want to get any paint on my new clothes. I only got them yesterday."

Ah, she must have been out *shopping* with her dad when I arrived round at hers the day before. But what was the point of wearing new trainers, new Kappas and a new fleece round here when she knew we were going to be decorating? Honestly, she was as bad as Rowan; *she'd* ended up wrecking her favourite red velvet mules by wearing them when Rolf and Winslet dragged us for a walk in the mud round Highgate Woods a couple of weeks ago.

"Anyway," said Kyra, wriggling her arms out of the fleece and then rooting around in one of the pockets for something "I thought I'd take Ricardo's tape round, so Sandie could get a listen. It's too funny, isn't it, Ally?"

Before I could say anything, Sandie barked out, "Don't bother! My ... my tape deck's broken!"

I glanced over at her pink plastic ghetto-blaster – out of which some DJ's voice was wittering away – and felt confused. Sandie hadn't mentioned it was broken.

"Yeah? Oh, well..." shrugged Kyra, slipping it back into her fleece pocket. "So, anyone decided what to wear for Fancy Dress Friday yet?"

"No, I haven't got a clue, really," I muttered, standing up and stamping on one leg that had gone to sleep, I'd been crouched down so long.

"Well, you and Sandie could always go as a pair of painters and decorators. You've got the outfits sorted already!" snickered Kyra, pointing out our blue-splodged old clothes, never mind our blue-splodged hands, faces and hair. "What do you think, Sandie?"

But Sandie said nothing, didn't even turn around. The only response Kyra got was a quick raise and drop of Sandie's shoulders.

"Whassup with her?" Kyra mouthed at me, shoving her thumb in Sandie's direction.

What could I say? I didn't know. I hadn't really known for *days* now what was up with her.

And now I *really* didn't know what was up with her … at the sound of a rattle of keys in the front door, Sandie's head spun around, her face white with shock.

"Oh, no!" she whispered, her voice so full of dread that I expected her to tell me Jack the Ripper had a spare set of keys to her house.

"It's only your mum and dad, isn't it?" I asked, bemused.

"But they weren't meant to be back yet!" she whispered urgently.

"Well, so what?" laughed Kyra.

"So … they don't know I'm painting my room!"

Kyra frowned, shooting a look at me that said, "Is she crazy, or what?"

Still, however weird Sandie had been, I knew that in this instance she wasn't being crazy. Mr and Mrs Walker loved the little-girl prettiness of this room, and I'd been amazed that they'd finally agreed to let her have her own way and redecorate. But if Sandie *hadn't* asked permission, then they were going to go *ballistic*.

"Sandra, darling, are you OK?" I heard her mother's cooing voice come towards the door. "It's just that there's a funny smell in here, like paint or—"

I've never seen anyone faint, but that day I saw someone *nearly* faint. Sandie's mum took one look at the petal-patterned walls and started sinking to the floor, like she was being sucked into a puddle of quicksand.

"*Sandra!*" her father bellowed at her as he struggled to keep his wife in an upright position. "How could you do this to your mother and me!"

Uh-oh. I think it was safe to say that they weren't big, big fans of those mutant daisies, then…

Chapter 14

THE BLAME GAME

Here's the thing. And it's a completely insane thing.

Mr and Mrs Walker blamed *me*.

Oh, yes.

You'd think I'd persuaded their daughter to become a lap-dancer or something instead of just coming up with the mutant-daisy concept. And when it came down to it, it wasn't as if it was *my* idea to paint the stupid room in the first place – not that they seemed very keen on listening to what I had to say anyway.

And another thing: I never realized how fast Kyra could run. When Sandie's parents started ranting, you never *saw* anyone move so fast. In fact, forget the leopard; Kyra Davies could easily make it into the *Guinness Book of World Records* as the fastest mammal on the planet. As soon as Mrs Walker opened with, "I've never seen anything so dreadful in my life!", all I could see of Kyra was a total *blur* as she made a grab for her fleece and disappeared out of the flat.

Thanks, Kyra.

That left me and Sandie to face the music on our own. (Yeah, so Kyra hadn't done any of the actual painting, but she could have stuck around and done some good PR for us, telling Mr and Mrs Walker that the look was so amazing that professional design teams would have charged a *fortune* to create it. Maybe.)

Well, at first – as soon as the blur that was Kyra had slammed the front door shut – I *assumed* that me and Sandie would be facing the music together. But oh, no. The only person doing *any* facing of *any* music was yours truly.

"This is an abomination!" Mr Walker boomed, looking from the walls to me.

I looked at the walls and couldn't see an abomination. OK, so now I was standing back from it, I appreciated that it was a bit splotchy and would definitely need a second coat of paint to get rid of the Barbie pink trying to shine through. But if you tried to imagine it finished, you'd have to admit it was much better than it was before. But maybe Mr Walker was the type of man who didn't have much imagination.

"Tell me, Ally, how would *your* father like it if you did this to your own room?!" Mrs Walker turned on me next, snivelling into a hankie.

"He– he– he'd really like it!" I replied, knowing that what I'd said was true, but also that it wasn't the answer Sandie's mum wanted.

"Well, *we* don't! And you've got no right to persuade Sandie to do something like this against our wishes!"

I was so shocked that my brain emptied of anything to say in reply.

"But, Mum, it's not Ally's fault!" I heard Sandie finally protest in my defence.

"Sandie, I think it would be best if you and Ally didn't see each other for a while," Mrs Walker suddenly announced, crumpling up her soggy tissue in her fist. "You're round at her house far too much, and the way you've been talking to me and your father lately, it's obvious that she's a bad influence."

That last insult did it. I'd never been so hurt in my life: I felt like she might as well have slapped me in the face – *and* given me a Chinese burn while she was at it.

I knew I was about to start crying, and there was no way I was going to give Mr and Mrs Walker the satisfaction of seeing me blub.

So I did a Kyra, and ran...

Fluffy was twitching in her sleep, jerking her black

and white legs backward and forward as if she was having a fantastic dream that involved chasing something small and edible.

Then again, I suppose she could have been having a hideous catty nightmare, reliving the moment when the brain-dead Dobermann in Fluffy's last home decided to have a bit of a chew on her tail.

Whether it was a dream or a nightmare, Fluffy didn't get a chance to continue with it – all of a sudden she awoke to find herself being lifted into the air and unceremoniously plopped down on to the cracked kitchen lino.

"You cats have *got* to stop jumping up on the table!" Grandma said to her, bending over and waggling her finger in Fluffy's whiskered face.

(Cats? Grandma would have flipped out the day that we all came down to Sunday breakfast to find Rolf on the table, snoring among the un-tidied-away plates and cutlery from the previous night's takeaway with his snout still lodged in a foil carton of leftover chicken tikka.)

Deeply offended at being removed from her comfy position and having a finger waved in her face, Fluffy turned on her furry heels, stuck her stump of a tail haughtily in the air and padded off to find somewhere new to dream and twitch.

"So unhygienic!" Grandma grumbled, flicking stray cat hairs off the table with a tea towel.

Not that it would make much difference. For every surface Grandma flicked, or floor she hoovered, there'd be two dogs and five cats merrily yawning, scratching and hair-shedding in all the other rooms in the house (well, apart from Linn's – she keeps hers so neat and pet-free that it's as sterile as a dentist's surgery. And about as cosy).

"That's better," Grandma announced, as she sat down, dishing out two huge pottery mugs of coffee (made by Mum: the mugs I mean, not the coffee) on to the long wooden table. "Now, what were you saying, Ally?"

It was about five o'clock on Monday evening, and Grandma had just finished helping Tor with his homework. And while he was through in the living room wearing his dolphin sanctuary T-shirt and watching *Pet Rescue*, and while my sisters were both in their rooms doing their homework (yeah, *right*), I'd taken the opportunity to talk to Grandma.

Sorry, make that *splurge* out all my *woes* to Grandma.

(I know that lots of people would go straight to their mum or their dad if something bad happened – i.e. your best mate's parents slagging you off – but in my case … it's just that having a mother who's in the remote Galapagos islands stroking endangered sea urchins or whatever, it kind of makes it *hard* to communicate your everyday problems. And then when it comes to Dad; well, I hadn't talked to Dad about what had happened with Sandie's parents, purely because of the Don't-Worry-Dad-He's-Got-Enough-To-Worry-About Pact that me, Rowan and Linn have. Of course we'd talk to him if something was really, *seriously* wrong with any of us, but generally, we try to sort things out between ourselves. With a little help from Grandma.)

"I was telling you about Sandie phoning last night," I reminded her.

"Ah, yes – to apologize for her parents' behaviour," Grandma nodded. "Well, that was sweet of her."

It might have been sweet of Sandie, but it hadn't made me feel any better. She'd phoned in the evening, and was whispering down the phone like a secret agent, so her mum and dad didn't hear. I think that's what hurt – it was all very well hearing Sandie saying how mortified she was at what had happened, but the very fact that she was telling me in *secret* meant that her parents didn't regret blasting off at me in the *least*.

"And what did Sandie say about it at school today?" Grandma asked, while inspecting the rim of her cup for stray hairs or paw prints before she sipped her coffee.

(I didn't bother telling her that *that* very mug had acted as a temporary home on Saturday night for Lumpy the goldfish, till Tor had washed and filled a spare fish bowl he'd found out in the shed, all dusty and covered with cobwebs. Lumpy had only languished in the mug for about ten minutes, and Tor *promised* he'd scrubbed the mug clean afterwards, but I decided information like that would just freak Grandma out too much. And right now I appreciated her being calm and *un*-freaked out.)

"Sandie didn't say much. She was just being super-nice and tiptoeing around me. And I didn't really want to talk about it," I replied.

'Cause I'd been scared that I might cry right there in the middle of a class at the injustice of it all, if you want to know the truth.

Grandma took a deep, reflective breath, and sighed it out before she spoke again.

"Well, from what you've told me before," she said, "Sandie's parents have always been nice to you, haven't they?"

"Well, yes, they've always been OK," I shrugged.

Suddenly, I realized that I'd never got on as well with Mr and Mrs Walker as I did with all my other friends' parents (including Kyra's, from the little I'd seen of them). I mean, Chloe's parents – they're always very friendly and chatty; Jen's are both into music (her dad plays in a local band); Kellie's mum's a real laugh, and Salma's mum and stepdad are always glad to see you, 'cause it means someone else is around to play with the twins and give them a break. And even Billy's mum – although she's a bit of a snob – is someone you could at least have a conversation with about clothes and fashion and stuff. But Mr and Mrs Walker?

Sitting at the kitchen table with Grandma, it struck me that they were so old-fashioned (and plain *old*) that I sometimes hadn't a clue what to say to them – and I think it was the same for them too.

"Mmm. Then it seems to me, from what you've said about Sandie complaining about them recently," Grandma announced, fixing me with a steady gaze through her thin-rimmed glasses, "that Sandie and her parents are having problems. But rather than shout at *Sandie*, they're taking it out on *you*."

"Taken what out?" I asked, scrunching up my face so much that I must have looked like Buffy – Tor's favourite black rat – when she was sniffing the air for rat treats (i.e. apples, carrots, passing victims she could bite and infect with the plague).

"Frustration," Grandma shrugged. "Maybe they're finding it difficult to accept that their precious little girl is growing up and is starting to be independent of them."

"Independent?" I squeaked.

It didn't feel much like Sandie was being independent to me. Not the way *she'd* been acting.

"OK, I know you've told me that she's been very clingy with you lately," Grandma conceded. "But that could be because things have been rocky for her at home."

"But if Sandie's having hassle with her parents, why wouldn't she tell me what was happening?" I frowned. "I *am* supposed to be her best friend!"

"Maybe she doesn't want to talk about it. Maybe she just wants to come around here, *be* with her best friend and forget about it," Grandma suggested. "And the fact that she's relying on you more at the moment; well, maybe that's why she's been acting a little jealous of Billy and Kyra and the others."

Urgh … that made me feel like I'd score a big, fat *zero* in a "How Good A Best Friend Are You?" quiz. Maybe – right now – Sandie just needed me to be supportive, no questions asked. And there was I, getting *irritated* by her and trying to see *less* of her.

"And then, of course, maybe there's something

else going on that Sandie can't tell you about,"
Grandma went on to suggest.

"Like what?" I asked her.

Out of the corner of my eye, I could see Tor
skulking into the room, holding something. For a
split-second, I hoped he wasn't going to announce
what Grandma's mug had been recently holding,
but that thought quickly vanished from my head –
I was too caught up with Grandma's insights on
What The Matter Was With Sandie.

"For example ... well, maybe Sandie's parents
are going through a bad patch, and they don't want
her to tell anyone. Something like that could be the
reason she's acting so unsettled at the moment."

Wow, my gran was good at this. If she wasn't
retired, I'd have suggested she should set up as a
counsellor or a psychiatrist or something. (Only
she's so practical, she'd probably end up telling
some of her flakier patients to stop being so whiney
and pull themselves together, and somehow I think
that's a big no-no in the world of counselling...)

"But what can I do to help her?" I asked my
super-psychiatrist gran.

By this time, Tor had silently joined us, sliding
himself on to one of the other chairs round the
table and setting down in front of him the small
plastic fish bowl containing Lumpy.

"I think you've got to be patient, Ally," said Grandma, taking another sip of her Lumpy-flavoured coffee. "Sandie's a shy little thing; I think you've just got to *be* there for her, and when she feels up to it she'll open up to you about what she's feeling."

Grandma was right. I *should* be a lovely, one hundred per cent supportive friend, and give her lots of opportunities to tell me what was going on – in her own time. And, like Grandma said, maybe Sandie's parents *were* having a hard time watching their daughter turn into an adult (I think if a Hans Christian Andersen-style fairy arrived on their doorstep one day and told them that it was possible for them to make a wish and keep Sandie as a cute little five year old for ever, they'd be signing on the enchanted dotted line, quick as a flash).

And, like Grandma *also* said, all Sandie's weirdness could be down to something awful like her parents arguing and maybe even splitting up, for all I knew.

Even though I didn't exactly adore Mr and Mrs Walker (especially after the way they'd talked to me the day before), I really hoped that wasn't what was wrong. But it might be... And so, from here on in, I would be a good and loyal friend to Sandie – no matter how creepy-clingy she was – and give her lots of chances to open up, whenever she was ready.

"And in the meantime, I wouldn't take it personally, what Sandie's parents said to you," Grandma smiled at me, while eyeing up the lopsided goldfish doing a circuit of its bowl. "I'm sure they regret it, and I'm sure they were upset about something that has nothing to do with you."

"Thanks, Grandma," I smiled back, sensing the knot of hurt (that had been there for the last thirty-six hours) slowly untangle in my stomach.

"Grandma…" said Tor, sensing a lull in our conversation.

"Yes, sweetheart?"

"You see my new goldfish?"

"Um, yes, dear," nodded Grandma, squinting at the very peculiar blob on Lumpy's side.

(If there was a goldfish version of Crufts, trust me: this fish would *not* win.)

"Well, I've got a name for it. A *special* name."

For a second, I was confused; I thought the thing had a name, then I remembered that Linn had come up with "Lumpy" after she'd first gawped at the fish when she'd come in from work on Saturday. It was a name that Tor had instantly taken deep, *deep* offence to.

"And what is that special name, Tor?" asked Grandma.

"I'm going to call him ... *Stanley*."

Aww... From the twinkle in his eye and the breathiness in his voice, it was obvious that Tor was bestowing a great gift on Grandma's boyfriend. Still, touched as the human Stanley might be, I could think of cooler animals to bear your name.

But, while having a sickly goldfish with a growth the size of another *fish* on its side might not seem like the most flattering compliment in the world to some people, coming from my little brother, of course, it was *highly* prestigious.

"Well, isn't that kind of you, Tor. Stanley *will* be pleased," Grandma nodded seriously.

Ha.

From where I was sitting, I could plainly see that the corner of her mouth was twitching, seriously in danger of transforming into a smile, which was why I immediately got up – giving Tor a quick pat on the shoulder – and tried to leave the room before either me or Grandma ruined my brother's grand gesture by giggling.

"Oh, Ally!" Grandma called after me, just as I walked out into the hall.

"What?" I grinned at her from the kitchen doorway.

"I meant what I said about Sandie's parents," she assured me, over the top of Tor's head. "I'm sure it was a one-off, and I'm sure it had nothing to do with you, really."

"Thanks," I nodded at her.

Thinking that was it, I went to walk away again, not realizing that Grandma still had one last thing to say.

"But if they ever talk to you in that tone again, Ally, you *must* tell me," she said sternly, "and I'll go round and have a word with them. Fair enough?"

"Yep," I nodded, giving her a quick thumbs-up and a little smile.

It's great to know you've got someone on your side. Specially someone like Grandma.

I would *hate* to be in Mr and Mrs Walker's shoes if she arrived on their doorstep to have a word about someone defaming one of *her* grandchildren.

And I would *love* to have a hidden camera to tape that...

Chapter 15

PERFECTLY SIMPLE (I WISH...)

It was Tuesday.

It was Design & Technology.

I had just heard that Warren Murphy had put together a revolutionary, movement-sensitive pond alarm that would instantly let parents know if their child had fallen in the water. He'd been planning on donating it to the craft fair on Saturday, but the teacher wouldn't allow it – Mr Bolan wanted to send it to *Tomorrow's World* and try and get a big international company to put it into production.

I looked at my Windowsill Bird Table and wondered why it was still so rubbish.

"Huh! What a show-off that Warren is, isn't he?" Kyra grumbled, sidling up to me on my left-hand side with her arms folded across her chest.

I noticed she had her ugly old lab-goggles balanced on her head at what my Grandma would call "a rakish angle", i.e. squint and somehow cool, while I looked like a total dork in mine.

"Mmm," I mumbled in reply, although I actually

thought Warren was probably a genius who in years to come would be a millionaire businessman like Richard Branson while we were all in our mid-thirties, still trying to repay student loans and working out whether there was enough left over for a new tube of lip gloss and a Big Mac with fries.

"I hate people like him, who think their lives are so *perfect*," Kyra narked, giving an oblivious Warren Murphy a dirty look.

"Yeah, well, we don't *know* that his life's perfect..." I replied, trying to be fair.

I mean, Warren was just one of those quiet boys in your class that you never get to know very well. He seemed nice and well balanced enough, but for all we knew his life could be really hard. Maybe his parents were disabled and he had to be their carer. Maybe his parents were hardened criminals and Warren was always on the verge of being taken into care. Maybe his parents were both Maths teachers – urgh! That really *would* be awful.

"Humph!" snorted Kyra, obviously not too happy with me giving the wrong response to her dig about Warren and his supposedly charmed life.

In fact, she was *so* put out, she kicked the work table with her foot. Hard.

"Careful!" said Sandie, who was sitting on a bench to my right.

Kyra hadn't been in danger of ruining any delicate creation of Sandie's; it's just that at that precise moment Sandie was using her craft knife to clean her nails, and one unexpected jolt of the table – care of Kyra – could very nearly have sent her to the casualty department of the Whittington Hospital.

("So, nurse, what seems to be the problem here?" "Well, doctor, this drongo of a kid was cleaning out the scuzz from under her nails with a razor-sharp knife, and got the thing rammed halfway down her finger!" "Good. Serves her right for being an idiot. Next!")

"What's up with you?" I asked Kyra, who was now swearing under her breath and hopping about on her one unbroken foot.

"My stupid, so-called mother!" she spat out.

Me and Sandie exchanged quick little glances.

"What's she done?" Sandie asked her, putting her craft knife down well out of harm's way.

"She was in her *usual* mess last night," Kyra bitched.

"Drunk?" I suggested, immediately envisaging Mrs Davies, chatting easily and warmly over the breakfast bar with me on Saturday.

"Of *course*, drunk. What else?" snarled Kyra. "So I tried to keep out of her way – I went to my room and started trying out different clothes and stuff for Friday."

"And...?" Sandie prompted her.

"*And* she came barging into my room without knocking –"

That didn't sound too shocking. Annoying, maybe, but not shocking.

"– and she took one look at what I was wearing and just started screaming at me that I looked like a slag!"

I went all hot and cold at the same time. I couldn't imagine what it must be like to have your mum talk to you like that.

"What did you say back to her?" I blinked at Kyra.

"Nothing! There's no talking to her when she's like that. I just had to go and get Dad – he's the only one who can calm her down when she's off on one."

Mrs Davies, with her perfectly blow-dried chestnut bob, her perfect make-up and clothes, sitting in her perfect hi-tech kitchen, being perfectly charming and smart.

Somehow, though I was shocked at what Kyra had just said, I was finding it really difficult to picture her mother tanking back loads of booze and totally losing it.

"God, I *hate* her sometimes!" Kyra half-growled.

"Kyra Davies!" Mr Bolan's voice boomed across the room.

Everyone, including the practically award-winning Warren Murphy, turned to stare at her.

Kyra sighed, knowing she was about to get a telling-off.

"Back to your own bench, please, Kyra, and save your proclamations about who you hate till breaktime, please!"

There was a shuffle of shoes across the dull grey lino as Kyra reluctantly slouched her way back to her own stool by a table at the back of the room.

"Ally, do you ... do you think Kyra's made that up?" whispered Sandie.

I glanced at her, wondering if Sandie was asking me because she knew *I* might be doubting it, or if she was saying it because it was a way for her to help put a wedge between me and Kyra, so she had me all to herself...

But I made my brain screech to a halt when it came up against that last thought. Like Grandma had said the night before, I had to be totally trusting of Sandie and not automatically think badly of her.

"I don't know," I whispered back, feeling rotten too for doubting Kyra.

But for now, Sandie – as my best friend – was more deserving of my loyalty.

In other words, call me flaky, but I just didn't think I had the energy to deal with both of my mates and their problems at once. *And* finish the stupid, wonky Windowsill Bird Table in time for the craft fair.

Chapter 16

TORTURE BY TICKLING

"And he's phoned Ally every night since then, desperate to find out what I thought of the tape!" Kyra boasted, lying back in the futon chair and putting her hands behind her head with a self-satisfied smirk.

"Yeah? Is that right, Ally?" Kellie asked me, wide-eyed.

"Mm-hmm," I nodded, since my mouth was too full of Quavers to talk properly.

It was Wednesday, and it was Jen's turn to shoo her parents and her sister out of the living room so we could have one of our Girls' Video Nights. Only it was turning into more of a Girls' Gossiping Night, since the video we'd got was a really duff comedy that was about as funny as having chicken-pox – and about as irritating.

Of course, it didn't help that we were round at Jen's place, with the TV that has a screen so small it would be perfect for a family of *ants* to watch.

"Like, he's phoned you *every* night?" said Salma,

widening her permanently sleepy-looking brown eyes in my direction.

I nodded again.

Oh, yes, lovesick Richie/Ricardo had phoned my house every, single, solitary night since I'd given his karaoke tape to Kyra. The first call had been on…

Saturday evening: Rowan had picked up the phone, and when I heard her mention his name, I had to run through and frantically mime that I didn't want to talk to him, and that she should pretend I was out. I couldn't help it; it had only been a couple of hours since I'd been howling out loud at his singing efforts in Kyra's bedroom, and I didn't trust myself not to explode into giggles the minute I heard his voice. I thought he might phone back, but I didn't reckon it would be so soon, as in…

Sunday evening: I'd picked up the phone about a second after I walked through the door, fresh from Sandie's house and being ranted at by her parents. Because of that, I was definitely in *no* danger of summoning up a smile, never mind a snigger, when I heard Richie/Ricardo say hello, but I wasn't in the mood to talk to him either. (All I *was* in the mood for was to hide away in my room and feel sorry for myself.) So I muttered something about being busy and I'd speak to him another time. Which happened to be…

Monday evening: The phone rang right after I'd left Grandma and our chat about life, the universe and Sandie. "Did Kyra like the tape? Will she go back out with me? What did she say?" he'd prattled down the line. If I was being honest, I'd have answered, "No, no, and you really *don't* want to know", but I couldn't bring myself to be that mean. So, all I said was that she was thinking about it. Which Kyra just about *killed* me for the next day. "Well, *I'm* not going to be the one to tell him to get lost!" I'd told her. So she promised me she'd call Richie/Ricardo that night, to put him out of his misery. Only, next thing, it was...

Tuesday evening: And he was on the phone again. Grandma took the call, when I'd gone to pick up Tor from his friend's house, where he was staying for tea. When I got Richie/Ricardo's message, I knew instantly that a) Kyra hadn't bothered getting in touch with him, and b) I wasn't going to call him back, since it would just be a rerun of all the other calls so far.

"He must really be in love with you!" Kellie smiled dreamily at Kyra.

"Mmm," shrugged Kyra, pretending it was no big deal to be thirteen years old and have a boy so crazy about you that he was pestering your mates with begging phone calls and recording slushy ballads for you.

"Does he sound really unhappy when he's talking to you, Ally?" Kellie turned and asked me, making it sound like Richie/Ricardo's unrequited love was just about the most romantic thing she ever heard (blee). "Does he sound, y'know, heartbroken?"

"Well, he sounds kind of *whiny*," I replied, wondering who in my family would be answering his call tonight, since I was out.

"Why don't you get it over with, Kyra? Why don't you just phone the guy and tell him he's chucked?" Chloe pointed out with typical Chloe bluntness.

I watched Kyra's face fall. It was as if she loved the drama of it all – she didn't want someone coming up with a straightforward answer to her problem. Being straightforward was no fun, where she was concerned.

Maybe it's the same with her mum, I thought, shaking my head as Sandie stuck a bowl of dry-roasted peanuts under my nose. *Maybe Kyra just has ordinary, everyday tiffs with her mum but blows them up into these dramatic drunken fights, just to make herself sound more interesting...*

But I didn't have time to dwell on that niggly little idea any further, because a gnome had just walked in the room.

"Where's your fishing rod?" yelped Chloe as we all burst out laughing at Jen.

"What do you mean?" asked Jen, blinking her dark, doll-like eyes at Chloe.

"Well, you're a garden gnome, aren't you?"

"I'm a *pixie*, I *told* you!" Jen insisted, her cheeks looking very pink against the green felt of her hat and tunic.

Poor Jen; she'd been working all weekend on her outfit for Fancy Dress Friday, and had been looking forward to giving us a sneak preview tonight – and all we were doing was giggling. But honestly, it was hard not to. She'd told us she'd been inspired by the Flower Fairies, that series of cute, Victorian-ish kids' paintings that are quite famous. But standing in her living-room doorway in head-to-toe green (including green tights and dyed-green cotton gym-shoes) she looked less like a Flower Fairy illustration and more like a courgette in the vegetable section at Tesco.

"I haven't quite finished it," Jen sulked, flopping down on the arm of the futon chair Kyra was sitting in. "I've still got to sew a pom-pom on the end of my hat."

Ah, a courgette with a pom-pom...

That was it; we were all off again.

"At least *my* costume's nearly finished!" Jen blurted out, to make herself heard above our sniggering. "What are *you* lot wearing?"

"My cousin came round with his ice-hockey kit last night, so I'm sorted!" Kellie grinned happily.

Kellie would look cute in a big, numbered shirt and helmet, but I wasn't sure how it would work. We'd all been to see Nev and his team play up at Ally Pally skating rink, and he was just about twice as tall and twice as *wide* as his little cousin.

"And I'm still going to go as a vampire!" Salma said with relish. "My sister got me these great plastic fangs from the joke shop she works next to in Camden!"

"That'll look really cool," said Chloe, "till you have to answer a question in class, and start *slavering* down your chin when you try to talk!"

"Well, I just won't talk, then!" smiled Salma. "What about you?"

"Got all my stuff ... well, apart from a horse!" Chloe stated.

Chloe was a mad Madonna fan, and looking through lots of her albums for inspiration, had finally decided that Madonna's cowgirl look would be the easiest to copy. Pity she hadn't gone for one of the raunchy ones – I'd love to have seen Mrs Fisher our hideous Year Head's face if Chloe had wandered along the corridor in a big pointy bra. (I don't suppose the boys at school would have minded that, either...)

"What about you, Sandie?" Jen the Courgette asked, gazing over at the sofa, where me and Sandie were both sitting.

"We're going as painter and decorators, aren't we?" Sandie smiled at me, as a wave of disappointment swooshed in my chest.

It was such a *lame* idea; Kyra had only said it as a passing joke on Sunday, but, since neither of us could come up with a better plan, we were stuck with turning up to school with paint-splattered clothes and brushes.

I just hoped the janitor didn't see and suppose we were from the council, and expect us to do up the canteen roof or something. But come to think of it, that would be a good excuse to skive Maths, I suppose...

"Kyra?" said Jen, turning her attention away from us, since our outfits were obviously *way* too dull to comment on.

"Can't tell you!" Kyra grinned.

"Aw, come on! Not fair!" Chloe moaned at her. "We've all told!"

"Nope," said Kyra, closing her eyes and shaking her head. "Not telling."

"Kyra! You've got to!" squealed the courgette on the arm of the chair, giving her a dig with her green elbow.

"Can't. If I told you, I'd have to kill you," Kyra replied infuriatingly.

And she *didn't* tell, even when we all piled on her, thumping her with cushions and tickling her to death.

"Nope," she panted breathlessly, as we gave her one last chance to talk before we poured the bag of Wotsits down her vest top.

Kyra and her strange little secrets … what *was* she like?

Chapter 17

ROWAN GETS GLOWING...

Sandie had been loads better over the last couple of days.

OK, so we'd gone shopping after school on Tuesday, and she'd ended up buying exactly the same magazine and nail varnish as I did. And last night at Jen's she was practically like my Siamese twin, she stuck so close by me (to the point where she gave Kellie a dirty look for nicking the seat next to me on the sofa when she nipped to the loo).

But, in my new spirit of serenity, I was *not* going to get narked by stuff like that. Oh no. Sandie was my best friend, and we'd get through this weird little patch, me and her, 'cause best friends do everything together.

Except...

Except I found myself up on the Broadway, after school on Thursday, all alone and with a desperate desire to find myself a costume for the next day that *wasn't* as brain-numbingly boring as the painter-and-decorator idea.

I'd only been planning to go to the supermarket and pick up a few things that Grandma had asked me to get, but the lure of all the charity shops was too much. It was just that it had suddenly occured to me that *I* was the one who'd come up with the Fancy Dress Friday idea in the first place, so people at school would *expect* me to wear something semi-decent.

You know, if I had a choice, my absolute fantasy fancy dress outfit would have been Michelle Pfeiffer's Catwoman costume from *Batman 2*. Since it was only made up of a patchwork of black vinyl, I guess I *could* have tried making it a) if I'd given myself enough time, and b) if I could actually *sew*. (Knowing my version of the art of sewing, all those patchwork pieces would have bulged and flopped all over the place. I'd probably end up looking less like a Catwoman the Super-Vixen and more like Catwoman the Bag-Lady.)

In case you think I was being totally impractical, it wasn't as if I'd expected to walk into the local Oxfam and find that Ms Pfeiffer had been passing and dropped in her unwanted black catsuit (I *wish*). But, fingers crossed, lurking among the bobbly jumpers and second-hand bric-a-brac, I hoped I might just find myself a last-minute lightning bolt of inspiration.

Wrong!

Three charity shops later and the closest I'd got to a possible costume was a hideous pink, shiny shell suit, straight out of the eighties. But I didn't *want* to be a joke (or a painter and decorator) when I walked through the school gates next day. I wanted to look cool. I wanted people to *gasp* at my gorgeousness and wish *they'd* come up with something that inspired. I wanted … the impossible.

Poo.

"Well, hello. Ally, isn't it?"

I stopped staring glumly at the pavement and glanced up to find a familiar, friendly face.

"Hello, Mrs Davies!" I smiled back.

"What are you up to today, then, Ally?" she beamed at me, her perfect chestnut bob drawn back into a smooth, stubby ponytail.

"Just doing some shopping. For my Grandma," I replied awkwardly, holding up a bag of groceries as if I expected Kyra's mum to inspect it.

I didn't want to tell her I'd been looking for fancy-dress outfits; not after what Kyra had said about their fight the other night.

If it had actually *happened*, of course.

And looking again at this nicely dressed, *nice* woman, I had that horrible feeling in my stomach again that Kyra might have been telling porky-pies about her, all the way down the line...

"What a lovely granddaughter you must be!" Mrs Davies commented, making me blush around the edges.

"Well, it's not just for her; it's for our tea," I blabbered, trying to let her know that I wasn't exactly a saint or anything. "Our Grandma makes our tea during the week, 'cause of Dad working and us all having homework and..."

I tapered off, realizing I wasn't making a very good job of explaining myself. I was nervous; it was hard to look this woman in the eyes, knowing that her daughter had been going around saying such wild stuff about her.

"And your mother?" asked Mrs Davies tentatively.

"Oh, she's away," I shrugged.

God, that was worse – that made it sound like Mum was in *prison* or something. I went to open my mouth and explain more, but it was all too complicated ("Mum went on holiday four years ago and never came back – but it's OK, we're all right about it! Sort of!"), so I left it and said nothing.

"Oh..." murmured Mrs Davies, sounding sorry for me.

Urgh, she really *did* think Mum was in prison.

Quickly, I scrabbled round my brain for something else to say.

"So ... are you coming to the craft fair on Saturday?" I asked her.

"Craft fair? What craft fair?" frowned Mrs Davies.

So Kyra hadn't even told her about it. What was *with* her? I was starting to feel really sorry for Mrs Davies.

"Our school's holding this big fund-raising craft fair," I explained. "Everyone's had to make something to sell at it. And me and Kyra and my friend Sandie are looking after one of the stalls."

Mrs Davies let a sigh escape from her lipsticked mouth and rolled her eyes.

"My daughter tells me *nothing*, Ally," she laughed ruefully. "But never mind. What time does it start?"

"Eleven o'clock. Till four. In the main school hall."

"Great! I'll look forward to seeing you there! But, Ally," she said, winking at me conspiratorially, "let's not tell Kyra! Let's make it a surprise when I turn up!"

Kyra seemed to have plenty of secrets, but now it felt quite nice to be sharing one with her mother.

And suddenly I felt quite excited: whatever the truth was about Kyra and her mum's problems, maybe, just *maybe*, I could help them get on better … starting with getting them together at the craft fair on Saturday.

"How's your bird table coming along, Ally Pally?" asked Dad, making a grab for the bread before Tor took it all to make a towering bread castle in the middle of the puddle of gravy on his plate.

"Don't ask," I groaned, thinking of the jumble of assorted *sticks* with my name on it sitting in the cupboard of the Design & Tech room. "In fact, just ask me another question."

"OK, then," smiled Dad. "So what's your outfit going to be for tomorrow?"

I let out a long, tortured moan and thumped my forehead down on the table, right beside my empty plate.

"Am I guessing here, or are you not too pleased with that either?" I heard Dad laugh.

Without removing my head from the table, I just gave him a fed-up grunt in reply. (Although I did feel slightly soothed by the small hand that was now stroking my neck and head. Tor knew it calmed down the animals when he did that, so he was trying it on me. Pity he had gravy on his fingers, though…)

"Ally's going as a painter and decorator," Linn

explained to him matter-of-factly. "She thinks it's a lousy idea and she's right."

"Thanks!" I muttered, raising my head and giving my sister a black look.

"Well, that doesn't sound too bad to me!" Dad said cheerfully. "What are you going to wear? Those white dungarees you see painters in?"

"*No*. She's going to dress up in *your* old shirt and *her* old tracksuit bottoms – the stuff she wore when she helped Sandie decorate her room on Sunday," Linn told him. "Oh, and for that authentic look, she's going to carry a *paintbrush*."

Said like that – with a layer of sarcasm spread all over it – it certainly was obvious that my outfit *stank*.

"Linn, don't tease your sister, please," said Grandma. "I'm sure Ally will look just … *fine* once she's all dressed up."

Oh no; even Grandma thought it was a crummy idea.

But while I was miserably glancing from Dad to Linn to Grandma and back again, I was missing something.

How could I have done that? How could I not have noticed the glow of excitement around Rowan? It wasn't till Tor nudged me and pointed his fork in her direction that I saw it: a glow that was invisible to everyone except those of us who know that Rowan's head is stuffed with mirrorballs and fairy lights and glittery things.

"Uh-oh…" I muttered.

"No, Ally! It'll be brilliant!" Rowan gushed, jumping up from her seat. "Come on – let's go up to my room, now! I've got a great idea!"

I didn't know if I trusted her, but then I didn't have much to lose.

"OK! You're on!" I nodded, following her out of the kitchen.

"Ally!" I heard Grandma call out.

"Yes?" I replied, pausing in the doorway.

"It's your turn to wash the dishes tonight, isn't it?"

"Oh, yeah…" I sighed, taking a step back into the room.

"Well, it's all right, dear," she smiled at me. "Linn will take your turn, won't you, Linn?"

"Er … sure," said Linn uncertainly, knowing that it was Grandma's way of making her pay for being so sarky to me.

"Thanks, Linn!" I said brightly.

Maybe it was just my big sister's tummy rumbling, but I could have sworn I heard her growl…

I didn't grin till I was safely out of her sight in the hallway. But before I could bound up the stairs after Rowan, I had to answer the phone. And before I could do *that*, I had to find it, since it was lost under the long-haired, black and white furriness of Fluffy.

"How can that be comfy?" I asked her, scooping her off the hall table and picking up the receiver.

"What?" came a boy's voice at the other end of the line.

"Hello?" I said, confused.

"Ally?"

"Richie? I mean, Ricardo?"

"Oh, right ... it *is* you. I thought I had the wrong number or something. What was that stuff about being comfy?"

"I was just ... look, it was just a cat-thing. It doesn't matter," I answered him, sounding a tiny bit irritable.

But that was because I knew what was coming next, and I didn't really have time to fob him off again – not when me and Rowan were on a mission to get me glammed up for tomorrow (and getting someone like me glammed up was going to take Rowan a long, *long* time).

"Oh. Anyway, Ally, I was just wondering, y'know ... has Kyra said anything yet?"

I bit my lip.

It wasn't up to me to tell him he was one hundred

per cent dumped with no chance of getting back together with her, but if *Kyra* wasn't going to tell him, then *someone* had to; i.e., little old me.

"Look, I'm sorry, but Kyra doesn't want to get back with you."

There was silence.

"Ever," I added.

More silence.

"Sorry," I repeated, in an embarrassed mumble.

I heard a kind of gasp and almost imagined poor Richie/Ricardo deflating like a party balloon.

"Uh … gotta go. See you, Ally," he said hurriedly, in a gulpy voice.

"Yeah, see you," I replied and hung up the phone.

Aw, poor Richie/Ricardo. It was all over. Me and my family would probably miss his nightly calls…

Not.

Chapter 18

OOOOH, BABEEE, BABEEEE!

Dad and Tor stood at the gate to witness the novelty.

Yep, me, Linn and Rowan were all going off to school together: well, there is safety in numbers when you're wearing fancy dress...

Not that you'd really have noticed in Linn's case.

"I thought you were supposed to be going as a witch?" I'd said to her, when she'd walked into the kitchen at breakfast time wearing her normal out-of-school uniform of black trousers, black top and smart black ankle-boots. Even her hair was the same: her (naturally wavy) blondish long bob was blow-dried *iron* straight.

"I *am* a witch!" she said as she grabbed a piece of peanut butter on toast from my plate.

I was tempted to say, "Yes, I *know* you are," but I was scared she'd whip the other slice of peanut butter on toast away from me too.

"Well, what kind of witch?" I demanded.

Secretly, I'd been looking forward to seeing her with a big false nose and *warts*.

"Sabrina the Teenage Witch, of course!" she grinned, pulling a soft toy black cat from behind her back.

"Hey! That's Tor's!" I pointed out.

Tor not only had a *real* animal collection that rivalled London zoo, he also had a *stuffed* animal collection that rivalled the soft-toy section at Hamley's. It was hard working out how there could be room for him in his bed, what with the contents of Noah's stuffed-animal Ark vying for space.

"It's OK," Linn sighed, "I *asked* him if I could borrow it before I took it."

So Sabrina the-very-ordinary-looking Teenage Witch (her cat sticking out of her bag) was on my left as we walked to school, while on my right-hand side was ... a psychedelic fairy.

Yep, Rowan was in heaven; I think she'd have happily handed over *all* her pocket money *every* week for the privilege of wearing fancy dress to school permanently.

She did look fantastic, though, with little white wings (natch) and this amazing skirt made up of layers and layers of day-glo-coloured netting. She also wore a clingy, silky, pink vest top, with pink tights to match, and on her feet were her latest purchase ("Six quid from the Indian shops in

Turnpike Lane, Ally! They'd cost a fortune in the West End!"): purple satin, flat mules, encrusted with spangly beading. She'd twisted her dark hair up into a messy bun and stuck in a cheap diamanté tiara. But the best bit, the bit that made Tor look so proud as we walked off, was the feathery pink cat-toy wand that she was waving graciously in the air...

"Have a good day, girls!" Dad called after us. "You all look great!"

I turned and waved at him and Tor, and saw my dad give me that same funny happy/sad smile he'd given me the night before, when I'd come down-stairs after Rowan had done her makeover on me.

But then I suppose it *must* have been a shock. Rowan described it as the hippy look, but basically I was going to Fancy Dress Friday disguised as my *mum*.

I liked it, though; I liked the swish of her long, layered cotton skirt as I strode along the pavement. I liked the feel of the silky soft, patterned Indian top I was wearing (which still smelt faintly of her favourite patchouli perfume), and the beads round my neck and wrists that jingle-jangled with every step. Rowan had done more plaits in my hair, and this morning she'd even painted a flower on my face. OK, so Mum had never done that (not that *we'd* seen!), but it seemed more authentic, like the stuff you sometimes see on telly about Woodstock, that famous old hippy festival in America. The only thing I was finding trouble with was the clogs...

"Oooh! You all right?" asked Rowan, catching me as I turned over on my ankle again.

"Yeah, but I knew I should have worn my trainers!" I muttered, trying once more to concentrate on walking.

"But they wouldn't have gone with the look!" Rowan protested, sending trickles of glitter powder flying into the air from her hair as she turned to stare at me.

"But this skirt's so long, no one can even *see* my feet!" I tried to tell her.

"*Alllleeeeeeeeeeeee!*"

"Hey look!" Linn pointed at the figure running to join us. "It's Handy Andy off *Changing Rooms*, isn't it? Oh, no, it's just Sandie!"

Automatically, I turned at waved at my friend, and then immediately noticed that she was slowing down as she got closer, the smile fading from her face. Sandie – dressed in her dad's paint-splattered sweatshirt and her own old leggings and trainers – wasn't looking at Linn and her non-existent witch outfit. And she wasn't staring at Rowan's potentially award-winning psychedelic fairy outfit (even if plenty of other people in the street were). No – she was staring at me. Ally the Hippy. Definitely *not* Ally the Painter and Decorator.

Uh-oh. I should have phoned her and told her, shouldn't I?

"Ally!" she burst out, tears twinkling in her eyes. "What are you wearing?!"

"It was just that last night … me and Rowan … we…"

"We were just mucking about with our mum's old clothes and came up with this!" Rowan jumped in, trying to explain.

"You look good, Sandie!" Linn said soothingly, sensing Sandie's outrage at my disloyalty. "I like the streak of blue paint on your face. Nice touch!"

"What?! That's not meant to be there!" Sandie panicked, rubbing blindly at her face with her hand. "Oh no … I was trying to get some blue paint on this old brush this morning, I must have got some on my…"

She turned her hand over and saw her Blue Babe fingertips. Then she turned her gaze to her side and saw matching Blue Babe fingerprints all over her new black schoolbag.

And, from the watery-eyed look she gave me, I felt like it was somehow all my fault.

"What a laugh today's going to be, eh?" Rowan

joked, linking arms with Sandie and speeding her along the pavement towards school.

They were brilliant, my sisters. All the way to school, they tried really hard to be chatty and friendly and upbeat. But it was no good; Sandie was no longer dressed as just a painter and decorator – she was a painter and decorator with a small black cloud trailing over her head…

Sandie looked tight-lipped and angry with me for the whole day, which was a complete bummer since the rest of it was such a laugh.

In our class alone, there was so much to snigger at. Apart from two Frankensteins, three ghosts and four black cats (thank goodness Michelle Pfeiffer didn't leave her catsuit in Oxfam after all – the Catwoman look would have been *so* passé, dahling!), there were some unexpected sights. Warren Murphy had gone up in all the girls' expectations by coming dressed as a fireman, while everyone was totally perplexed by Katie Pearson until she explained that the huge bobbly *thing* she was sewn into was supposed to be a *bean*bag. (The bobbles came courtesy of about forty under-inflated balloons in-between the two sheets she had zipped together around her. We all sussed out they were balloons when she sat down and popped loudly in our first lesson.)

Nearly all our teachers got in the spirit, too. Of the ones who taught our year, the best scores, in ascending order (according to me and my friends), went like this...

Fifth place – Mr Horace (Maths): who came as footballer (a slightly disappointing effort).

Fourth place – Mr Samuels (English): a schoolboy (must try harder).

Third place – Miss Kyriacou (Science): a Lollipop lady (a big improvement on her usual achievements).

Second place – Miss Thomson (History): a flamenco dancer (well done; good use of imagination).

First place – Mr Matthews (French): Austin Powers (excellent work!).

(By the way, no surprises for guessing that the only teacher not to join in was sour prune Mrs Fisher. I mean, our headteacher, Mr Bashir, even *he* spent the day swooshing along the corridors dressed as an old-fashioned headmaster, with a long black cape, a mortarboard and a *cane*, for goodness sake.)

My friends all looked great too. Salma did a Linn and wore all black, but with a gallon of black eyeliner, blood-red lipstick and her speciality plastic fangs, she was a *very* cool vampire. Chloe wore a

Stetson, jeans and cowboy boots, and with her red hair done up in two plaits was more like Woody's girlie sidekick in *Toy Story 2* than Madonna, but still pulled it off. Kellie's mum had done a great job of tacking up (and in) her cousin Nev's ice-hockey gear, and Kellie was kind of *frightening* when she brandished her hockey stick and roared through the grille in her helmet. Well, it made Sandie jump, anyway (which made a nice change from her throwing me dirty and disappointed looks).

Jen's costume was still ... *green*, but everyone seemed to accept that she was a pixie rather than a courgette, so that was a bit of a triumph.

And Kyra? Well, Kyra made all the boys in our class – wait a minute, make that all the boys in *school* – sit up and notice her. Wearing her hair loose and curly along with flared trousers and a spangly halterneck top, she spent the whole day talking in a loud and lairy Northern-ish accent. Oh, yes, she was Scary Spice and no mistake.

"Thank you," said Miss Thomson (aka the flamenco dancer), taking Kyra's proffered mosaic vase for the craft fair.

"Awwwright! No problem!" Kyra had screeched in a throaty half-Mancunian, half-Liverpudlian drawl.

Part of me was fascinated by how confident Kyra was about pulling her one-of-the-Spice-Girls look off, and the other part of me was apprehensive, worried about catching her eye in case she read my hippy-chick mind and found out that her mum was planning a surprise visit next day.

And yet *another* part of me – a part that I was trying to ignore in the excitement of the whole day – was depressed by the fact that my Windowsill Bird Table was still such a pathetic sight that I couldn't *bear* to hand it in yet. The only bit of luck was that, since I was running one of the stalls at the fair, I could take the stupid thing along next day, rather than turn over my disaster to Miss Thomson now, in front of everyone.

And that at least gave me a chance to take it home with me after school and try to fix it or paint it (or take a *flame*thrower to it); *any*thing that might make it marginally more attractive to a potential buyer.

Talk about hoping for a miracle…

But for now – whatever we were dressed up as – it was last period and Mr No-Fun Horace was (pointlessly) trying to fill our heads full of Maths.

"How does he expect us to concentrate while we have to stare at those horrible, knobbly knees of his in those football shorts?" I muttered to Sandie, expecting a stifled giggle – or at least a smile – but Sandie wasn't playing.

"Hmm," she muttered back, pretending to pay tons of attention (fnar!) to the exciting algebra problem Mr Horace was scribbling on the board.

Wow – she must have been so mad at me for not coming dressed as her painter and decorator twin. But I'm sorry – it wasn't as if it could only work as a double act, like Mulder & Scully or Wallace & Gromit or something.

I stared down at the empty pages in front of me, my pencil hovering above the blank lines, and silently cursed Sandie and her little black cloud. For all my positive vibes this week, she'd managed to cast a total downer over the whole of the day, with her pursed-up lips and hurt scowls. And as soon as the bell went, no matter what Grandma had said way back on Monday, I was going to walk away from Sandie and all her stupid sulks. Oh yes, I was most definitely—

"Babeeeee! It's yoooooo!"

I recognized the voice straight away: thin, warbly and trying too hard... Omigod. All heads had turned to look out of the window, and there he was – Richie/Ricardo – crooning away in the schoolyard, with a ghetto-blaster by his side.

"Yeah, girl! It's you-ooooooo! Oh, Kyra! It's true-oooooo-oooo-oooooo!" he "sang", as everyone inside our classroom – including Mr Horace – gazed outside with their jaws hitting the floor.

"Jeez!" I heard Kyra yelp from a few rows behind me.

"Eeek!" I yelped myself, when I *also* recognized the embarrassed-looking boy in the back-to-front baseball cap who was hovering beside the ghetto-blaster and Richie/Ricardo.

What *was* Billy playing at?

Chapter 19

PINK, I THINK

"Looks like they're back together, then!" said Billy.

"Oh, I don't know…" I shrugged. "I think Kyra's still thinking about it."

There; *that* got even Sandie smiling.

There wasn't actually much doubt that Kyra and Richie/Ricardo were officially "on" again; not from the way Scary Spice and him were snogging on the next park bench along.

It was after school, and Sandie (who'd been too entertained by the schoolyard karaoke to keep up her huffy mood), Billy and I were sitting on another of the benches that lined this particular sweeping entrance into Alexandra Palace.

Earlier, Richie/Ricardo (and Billy for that matter) had had a lucky escape. Before anything bad had happened to them – like Mrs Fisher storming out out of school and doing a citizen's arrest on them or something – the end-of-day bell had rung. Everyone had poured out of the building, desperate to take a closer look at the yodelling lunatic outside (only I think a lot of the girls were pretty impressed – you have to remember that Richie/Ricardo is good-looking, even if he *is* a berk). But no-one moved faster than Kyra Spice, who'd kept up her record as super-sprinter and bolted through the main door and into Richie/Ricardo's arms before half our class had even finished putting their books away in their bags.

"How did Richie talk you into helping him, Billy?" I asked, turning my gaze away from the snoggers before they made me feel too queasy.

"He promised me a month's loan of *Escape from Monkey Island*," shrugged Billy.

Silly me. There I was, thinking he might say something like, "Because Richie's my mate, and he needed my support", or "Well, it was all for love", but no – I was forgetting that it was Billy Stevenson I was talking to. And I should have guessed that bribery and a computer game would have more to do with Billy helping out than things as stupid and soppy as friendship and love.

"Yeah, anyway, Richie persuaded me to skive off our last class, so we could come on down here and surprise Kyra," he explained, playing with the knobs on the ghetto-blaster that was perched next to him on the bench.

"But how did you know where to set up?" asked

Sandie. "How did you know *that* bit of the yard was closest to our classroom?"

"Richie didn't have a clue," said Billy, accidently flicking the radio on and letting a blast of some drum 'n' bass track practically *deafen* us. "Oops, sorry!"

I reached over and turned it off for him.

(I noticed that the noise hadn't disturbed Kyra and Richie/Ricardo. I think a passing lorry-load of tap-dancing nuns setting off fireworks wouldn't have distracted *them* from each other.)

"But then," Billy continued, now that we could hear him again, "when we got to your school, I remembered Ally saying that last thing on Friday she'd be staring out of the window at the shops, just counting the minutes to escape ... and so that's how I knew it had to be one of the classes on *that* side of the building."

"Hey, that's smart thinking ... for *you*," I grinned, walloping him on the arm.

"Ouch!" he moaned, rubbing the spot, even though I knew I hadn't hit him that *hard*. "Well, Ally, I *was* going to tell you you looked really nice, dressed up like that, but I won't *bother* now..."

Aw, sweet! Billy giving me a compliment! (Almost...)

"Sorry!" I grinned, bending forward and

pretending to kiss his arm better.

"Gerrofff!" he yelped, blushing and laughing.

"Stop wiping at it! I didn't really kiss you!" I teased him. "And even if I did, it's not poisonous!"

"Dunno about that!" Billy grinned. "Anyway, what's in the bag?"

He pointed down at the plastic carrier that had fallen over, revealing the top of my Windowsill Bird Table.

"It's just a ... a *thing* I'm making," I shrugged, grabbing the bag and trying to hold it closed.

I felt very sensitive about this particular disaster and didn't particularly fancy Billy teasing me about it, which he would – guaranteed – given half a chance.

"Show me!" he laughed, making a grab for it.

"No!" I snapped, standing up and backing away from him. "Anyway, I'd better go – I've got to see Rowan about something..."

Oh, yes, I had to see Rowan about something, all right. Earlier in the day, I'd decided that as she'd done such a good job of my fancy-dress outfit she could maybe help me again tonight – and turn this awful clump of firewood into a thing of beauty...

Ha.

But Rowan couldn't help. It's not that she didn't

want to; it's just that she wasn't around. The psychedelic fairy had fluttered up to her mate Von's house after school (to show off her costume), and phoned later to say she was staying over.

Linn was out too, and Tor – while ace at making sculptures from food – wasn't much good at stuff to do with wood and hammers.

Dad and Grandma weren't a lot of help either; they just kept telling me that the bird table looked fine, and didn't do a very convincing job of hiding the fact that they were blatantly *lying*.

"Of course, you *could* always paint it. Maybe that would brighten it up!" Grandma suggested gingerly, for fear of offending me.

I didn't see how *painting* it was going to make the bird table look any less wonky and rubbish, but after a while (and out of sheer desperation) I ended up rummaging through the big attic store-room that lay between mine and Linn's bedrooms, and came out with a leftover tin of raspberry-pink emulsion, last used on Rowan's walls.

And so this morning I woke up, full of lazy Saturday-no-school happiness, and then sat bolt upright – wondering...

1) Why the room was so cold
2) Why I had a headache, and...
3) Why I had a feeling I had to be somewhere.

Slowly, the answers came to my stupidly sleepy head:

1) The room was cold because I'd kept the window open all night, so paint fumes from my drying bird table (on newspapers in the middle of my room) didn't asphyxiate me while I slept.

2) The paint fumes hadn't killed me (as far as I could tell), but they had been rank enough to make my head pound like someone had been hammering on it all night with a road drill.

3) I had to be somewhere, all right – behind a stall at a craft fair, in under an hour. And before that I'd have to shower, get dressed, and check that I had a "craft" I could enter without having to put a paper bag over my head to hide my shame.

Speaking of which...

Very slowly (like that would make a difference!), I turned my head and peeked at the vision of pinkness on the floor.

Actually, it looked kind of ... *cute*.

To be honest, I don't think any sane bird would have gone near it in a million years, but as a wobbly, kitsch little shelf-thing – maybe with a big fat candle on top of it – it *might* just work...

"*Yes!*" I said out loud, chucking back my duvet and bounding out of bed.

I walked over to the window and gazed out at

my namesake, Alexandra Palace, perched there on top of the hill, and smiled.

So, there was still lots of weirdness in my life. So, I still didn't get why Sandie was so moody, or why her parents ranted at me like they did. So, I didn't understand what was really going on with Kyra and her mum, and – most weird of all – why Kyra had got totally suckered into going back out with sleaze-boy Richie/Ricardo.

So what. Suddenly, none of it seemed to matter. Not when I had a Pink Thing I could take to the craft fair! A Pink Thing that someone might think was cute and kitsch enough to buy! Everything was going to be all right!

I plonked myself down on my chair and walloped my feet up on the desk, taking a deep, contented breath of Crouch End air in my lungs as I stared at the gorgeousness that was Ally Pally and stretched back…

…and back, and back, till my chair toppled towards the floor (oh, yes, with me in it).

Lucky, really, that there was a Pink Thing there to break my fall, or I could have *really* hurt myself…

After panicking for, ooooh, a good five minutes, I finally sat down cross-legged on my bed and deliberately stopped myself staring at the pile of pink splinters on the floor.

"What am I going to do?" I muttered, trying to get my breathing under control.

And then a funny thing happened. OK, two funny things; but I knew they were a sign, even if one could be explained away by the breeze drifting through the window and the other by our dog Winslet's insatiable desire to *steal*. It was the fact that they both happened at once that meant they were a sign...

So there I was, trying to stop myself from getting my head all twisty with panic, when I heard a tiny flutter, flutter, *thunk*. And there at my feet was a photo of Mum – one that I kept pinned to the big map of the world on my wall. She'd sent it from somewhere in Australia (I forget where), and she was pointing to a T-shirt she was wearing with a mad swirly pattern on it that she'd designed and painted herself. (That was how she made enough money to keep travelling: making and selling T-shirts and stuff.)

Just as I was smiling back down at her, I heard a determined thud as my bedroom door was head-butted open. In came Winslet – oblivious to me since I was sitting so still – clutching something in her determined little jaws and heading straight under my bed with her latest Precious Find. To chew to bits, naturally.

"Whoa!" I called out, as I scooped down and grabbed her by the scruff of the neck before she disappeared out of view.

Two startled brown eyes looked back into mine, and – knowing she'd been nabbed – Winslet automatically opened her jaws and let whatever it was plop to the floor.

I gave her a quick pat on the head to show it wasn't personal, then inspected her latest treasure. It looked like some kind of fish, but not of the edible type. It was made of clay ... in fact, when I looked closer, it could easily have been a dolphin, if you squinted your eyes a bit. And it was definitely one of Mum's bits of art.

Then I remembered; Mum made so much stuff (paintings, collages, pottery) that even in our big, rambling, falling-down house there wasn't enough room to have all of it on show. That's why some of the things she'd made over the years were kept in a couple of big boxes in the attic storeroom. And, last night, after rooting around for the paint, I probably hadn't closed the door properly, letting our small petty criminal of a dog spot an ideal pickpocketing opportunity (pickboxing opportunity?).

I looked down at the quirky statuette thing and

suddenly had the weirdest feeling, as if a cold finger had trailed right up my spine.

"Am I supposed to take this, Mum?" I blinked at her smiling face in the photo. "Can I put this in the craft fair?"

Her face didn't change, her wavy, light hair didn't move. But another waft of wind came through the window and made the photo flutter along the threadbare carpet.

"I'll take that as a yes," I smiled back at her, thrilled that Mum had somehow managed to come to my rescue.

I returned the favour by leaping off the bed and grabbing the fluttering photo before Winslet – who sees every moving thing as something to chase and chew – got her little hairy paws on it…

Chapter 20

A SURPRISE AND TWO SHOCKS...

"Are you sure it's meant to be a dolphin?" Kyra asked for the sixty millionth time, holding up the dolphin and frowning at it. "Are you sure it's not a seal? Or a really fat slug?"

OK, so she didn't realize that she was slagging off my mother's artwork (mainly because I'd lied and said I did it myself, at home). But to be honest, I was beginning to wonder the same thing myself, especially since dolphins were meant to be so popular, and especially now it was half-past three and it was one of the last things remaining unsold on our stall, along with a pair of hand-knitted stripy socks (in what looked like different sizes) and a really terrible poem about death that one of the sixth-formers had written in blood-red ink and framed (in a funereal-black border, of course).

Maybe Mum's sculpture *wasn't* a dolphin, of course. It *was* a funny, blobby sort of shape. And the two eyes didn't *really* match up. And the fin on the top *did* look more like a hump...

It had been a busy day for me and Sandie and Kyra at the craft fair. Not just because we'd sold lots of stuff, but because we'd had so many visitors. Billy had come and hung out for a bit, and I was really glad that he'd actually put his hand in his pocket for a good cause – even if he *had* eaten the entire chocolate cake by the time he'd finally found our stall. Then there'd been Chloe and everyone, come for a nosey and a chat and to buy some raffle tickets. Grandma had done her bit too, turning up and forking out a fiver for a set of gingham napkins off our stall.

I would have been really grateful to her, only she'd ended up picking up the "dolphin" and laughing at it – like a lot of people had done today, actually. I didn't have the heart to tell her it was her own long-lost daughter's handiwork (or the nerve to confess I'd stolen it...).

"Or maybe it's a short, fat eel..." Kyra teased me, sticking the sculpture back down on the table.

"Look, I told you, it's a dolphin, Kyra, OK?" I said emphatically, even though I wasn't convinced.

"Um, Ally?" said Sandie, tugging at my sleeve, to get my attention.

"Huh?" I replied, swivelling round to face her and presuming she just wanted to check a price with me or whatever.

"Mum and Dad..." she mumbled, pink-faced and pointing to the couple on the other side of the counter.

"Oh," I whispered, feeling myself go pink as I stared at Mr and Mrs Walker.

It was the first time I'd seen them since ... well, you know what since. I didn't want to humiliate myself by remembering their horrible accusations out loud.

"Oh, Ally!" her mother gushed at me, surprising me by looking very dewy-eyed.

"Uh, yes," her dad coughed. "Alexandra, we – my wife and I –"

I knew that they were married. He didn't exactly have to spell that out for me.

"– uh, well, we're both very, very sorry for the way we spoke to you on Sunday."

I shuffled my feet around and didn't know what to say or where to look. It's not often that a thirteen-year-old girl finds herself in the position of having two adults apologizing to her. No, make that *grovelling* to her.

"We really didn't mean it, Ally! Any of it!" Sandie's mum twittered.

I glanced sideways and saw that Sandie was blushing and shuffling as much as I was.

"It's just that things have been so ... well,

emotional for us lately, as a family, I mean!" Mrs Walker babbled on.

I didn't know what she was trying to tell me – and, right then, I couldn't concentrate on figuring it out anyway, because something truly terrible was about to happen and I could see it coming...

The first indication was that Kyra had gone wildly pale (well, as pale as her soft-brown skin could go).

Then I turned my head towards the commotion in the hall – trying to see what everyone was staring at, or who exactly.

Then I saw the woman, her hair a tangle of chestnut-brown frizz, stumbling and crashing into stalls as she made her way towards us, all eyes superglued to her.

Then I saw her trembling but well-manicured hand reach out and grab the socks from our stall.

"What? Is thish a joke? Kyra, do you seriously expec' someone to buy this crap?!" the woman babbled, slurring over her words.

"An' this?" she added, hauling Mum's dolphin in the air. "What the hell is this supposed to be?"

Mrs Davies looked, well, not like the perfect Mrs Davies I'd met at her house last Saturday and in the street a couple of days ago. *This* Mrs Davies had her shirt buttoned up wrong, her cardie falling off one shoulder, smudged mascara and a face so twisted and mocking that I hardly recognized her.

"Eh?" she yelled at me, practically pushing the dolphin under my nose. "D'you know wha' this is?"

To one side of me, I sensed Sandie freeze solid, and on the other side of the table, her parents were doing much the same. I glanced at Kyra and saw that she was scrabbling in her jacket pocket for her mobile phone.

"Do *you* know wha' this is supposed to be?" Mrs Davies said mockingly, wafting the dolphin ominously close to Sandie's mum's nose this time.

"No, I don't. Sorry," I heard Mrs Walker twitter, while in the background Kyra was whispering savagely, "*Now!* You've got to come right *now*, Dad!"

"It's … it's a d-dolphin," I stammered, trying to pacify the drunken Mrs Davies.

Not that she took a blind bit of notice of me.

"What are *you* lookin' at?" Kyra's mum snarled at Mrs Walker. "Think you're somethin' special, because of *that*?!"

For some reason, she was pointing at Sandie's mum's stomach.

"How dare you!" Sandie's dad suddenly barked at Mrs Davies. "How dare you talk to my wife like that, in her condition!"

Condition…? I glanced at Sandie, who gave me

a "See? *This* is what's going on!" look, then turned my gaze back and noticed – for the first time – her mother's gently bulging tummy.

Now, I may have got it wrong, but I don't think that bulge was down to her eating one too many takeaway pizzas. Still, I couldn't quite bring myself to believe that Sandie's mum was pregnant...

Chapter 21

SECRETS, AND *REASONS* FOR SECRETS

There were clatters and bangs and tinklings going on all over the school hall as stalls were dismantled and takings were counted.

Kyra, Sandie and I had packed up early, of course, *partly* because we had nothing much left to sell and *mostly* because of Kyra's mum causing such a scene.

Poor Kyra; Miss Thomson and Mr Bashir himself had come over to try and quiet the argument that was raging between Kyra's mum and Sandie's parents. It had all ended as quickly as it had started, though, when Kyra's tall, handsome dad came hurrying into the hall and spirited her protesting mum away.

"You stay here with your friends," Mr Davies had said to Kyra. "It'll give me a chance to get your mum calmed down..."

After that, Sandie's parents had hurried off too (because the stress wasn't doing Mrs Walker any good, "in her condition").

That left me, Kyra and Sandie, all three of us

pretty shaken by what had just happened. Not sure what to say or do, I automatically began to take down the stall. Following my lead, Kyra sat down to count out the money, while Sandie helped me by unscrewing the legs at the other end of the table.

Twenty minutes later, we found ourselves sitting on the steps that led to the stage – me in the middle, between Kyra and Sandie – partially hidden away from the chatter and confusion going on in the rest of the school hall.

"You know something?" Kyra broke the silence, without meeting our eyes. "I never knew what set her off with her drinking till recently."

"What is it, then?" I asked her, feeling horribly guilty for ever having suspected her of lying.

"When I was nine, Mum was expecting another baby, but she had a miscarriage."

"Oh," I said quietly.

What a *weird* thought – to have *nearly* had a brother or sister, only he or she never arrived...

"Lots of women have miscarriages," Kyra shrugged, "only it usually happens early on, Dad says. But in my mum's case, she was pretty big –" Kyra held her hand out to indicate a very pregnant tummy, "and so it was a lot harder for her to get over. And she didn't. Get over it, I mean. That's why she started drinking, just to cover up how depressed she was. And it's never got any better."

That was *so* sad. Poor Mrs Davies. But I was glad Kyra had told us; it made me less scared of what I'd just seen this afternoon.

"Was that … was that something to do with why she was yelling at my mum?" Sandie asked in a whisper.

"Yeah, I think so," Kyra nodded. "Dad says it can really upset her, seeing women who are pregnant."

The whole situation kind of freaked me out, but at least I felt I understood what was going on in Kyra's world a lot better. *Now* I needed to understand what was going on with Sandie…

"Why didn't you tell me your mum was pregnant?" I quizzed her.

"Her and Dad only told me a couple of weeks ago, and then they made me promise not to tell anyone," she burbled, twisting her hands together into a knot.

"But why not? Weren't they happy about it?" I asked.

I also wanted to ask how it was possible that they could even *have* a baby, they seemed so old. But that would have sounded too rude, whatever way I put it.

"Dad told me that because Mum's thirty-seven—"

"Your mum's *thirty-seven*?" I blurted out in surprise before I could stop myself.

Wow – that meant she was only a couple of years older than my mum and a couple of years younger than my dad, and *my* parents didn't look particularly old at *all*. Isn't it funny how the way people dress and act can make them seem *ancient*?

"Yeah, anyway," Sandie continued, "because Mum's thirty-seven, the hospital like you to get all these tests done, just to check the baby is all right. And Mum and Dad wanted to wait for the results of all that stuff before they started telling everyone."

"And *is* it all right?" Kyra leant forward and asked her. "The baby?"

"Yeah," Sandie sighed, sounding not too thrilled.

"Are you OK about it? The baby coming, I mean?" I asked her stupidly.

Of *course* she wasn't OK about it.

That's why she'd been slagging off her parents so much recently and got all creeped out by the idea of older people getting romantic – like the whole thing with Grandma and Stanley. OK, so Mrs and Mrs Walker weren't exactly as old as Grandma, but Sandie was obviously finding it a bit hard to get her head around the physical idea of *how* her parents had actually come to be having another baby.

"I just didn't think my parents, y'know ... *did* it," said Sandie, sounding horribly embarrassed.

Her pale cheeks got a little pink at that point, and I felt mine go a bit flushed too.

(Well, it *is* a weird thought. Parents and ... *you* know.)

"And then, since they told me," Sandie sniffed, suddenly sounding ominously tearful, "well, all they can speak about is the baby, the baby, the baby. It's like they couldn't care less about *me* any more."

("See?" said Grandma, when I told her about it later. "*That's* why she was so clingy: because she felt pushed out by her parents!")

Then I realized that I was hearing sniffing in stereo – Kyra was at it now too.

"Hey, you guys, it's going to be all right!" I tried to say cheerfully, wrapping an arm around each of them and giving them both a hug at once.

I didn't know *how* exactly it would be all right, but what else could I say?

Whatever, it hadn't made either of them feel any better. Kyra and Sandie both looked *totally* miserable.

OK, this called for drastic action...

"*Oooooh, babeeeee, it's gonna be alllll rigghhhhht!*" I warbled, doing my best impression of Richie/ Ricardo's karaoke tape.

Kyra and Sandie both stared at me as if I gone *mental*, then started – hurrah! – to giggle.

That was more like it!

And you know something? I was right, even if I didn't know it at the time. Everything did work out better. After the business at the craft fair, Sandie's mum and dad went back to being super-protective of her, smothering her in love, and even buying her some new furniture to go with her mutant-daisy walls.

And Kyra? Well, her mum was so mortified at showing Kyra up at school (something she'd never, *ever* done before – mainly because Kyra kept her at arm's-length) that she finally decided to go for counselling, to help her get over her sadness and the drinking that was linked with it. "She's getting on OK," Kyra said, last time I asked her about it, though I noticed she was keeping her fingers crossed when she spoke...

You know another thing that happened after that craft fair? I found out something about my mum. Something I've never told the rest of my family.

Oh, yes; that day on the stall it had suddenly occurred to me – the awful truth. The awful truth that my mum, as an artist, is ... well, isn't very *good*.

It's true! And I'm not just talking about the dolphin/slug-thing that no one wanted to buy. It's *all* the oddball paintings and wobbly pots and wonky sculptures dotted around the whole house. *None* of them are much cop.

But it doesn't matter – I still love every oddball, wonky, wobbly one of them, just because my lovely mum made them.

And, who knows, maybe she'd have liked that stupid Leaning Tower of Pink Bird Table I made. Maybe it's just the sort of thing *she'd* have come up with, given a few bits of wood and a hammer...

See ya. :c)

PS This is *strictly* between you and me, but the mutant daisies on Sandie's walls? Next time I went round there, I realized they looked *awful*. So don't try them at home. (And *don't* tell Sandie I said so. *Or* her parents. *Or* Rowan, seeing as it was her idea in the first place...)

Coming soon:

Boys, Brothers and Jelly-Belly Dancing

Girls and boys can never be proper friends.

What a load of cobblers...

Honestly, Kyra Davies has a one-track mind! I thought to myself, as I ambled home from the park, twirling the piece of paper with Alfie's name on around in my fingers. *Just 'cause she only sees boys as potential snoggees, she thinks that goes for* everyone...

Well, she was wrong. I mean, half the world is filled with blokes, right? And you can't fancy them *all*, so that means there's plenty left over to be potential mates.

So, how do you tell the difference? How do you know which category (i.e. Fancying or Friendship) a lad fits into? Well here's my theory: if you can speak to a boy as easily as a girl, he's mate-material. But if you turn into a tongue-tied, bumbling geek with a brain of mush in front of a lad, then he's in the Fancying category.

And if there was one person guaranteed to turn me into a bumbling, tongue-tied geek with a brain of mush, it was the person whose name was slithering through my fingers right now.

Alfie, Alfie, Alfie...

How many nights had I lain awake running his name through my mind?

Answer: more times than there are stars in the sky. Probably.

Ally, Ally, Ally...

How many nights had Alfie lain awake running my name through his mind?

Answer: never. Almost definitely.

Bummer.

Of course, apart from boys of the fancying or friendship variety, there's *another* category: the ones you're related to. As I got closer to the house, all thoughts of Alfie slipped from my mind as I tried to figure out what my little brother was up to. From my angle, I could just make out Tor in our tiny, overgrown front garden, peering at a removal van that was parked outside the house next door. Every couple of seconds, I could see Rolf's head too, as he bounced up and down to try and see whatever was holding his human buddy's attention.

"Gotcha!" I roared, after slipping silently though the gate (a miracle, with that squeaky old pile of wood and rusty hinges) and pouncing on my brother.

"Ally!" he yelped. "I – I *knew* it was you!"

It was only a white lie, and it was quite funny really, seeing how caught-in-the-act red-faced Tor was.

"What are you doing?" I asked, hunkering down and joining him and Rolf behind their hideaway hedging.

It was quite nice down there; like a secret world. Hidden under the bushes were clumps of yellow and white flowers, bravely struggling to grow in the shade, and a whole bunch of sparkly glass marbles that were half buried at the root of the prickly bush I was avoiding getting too close to. For about half a second I wondered how those marbles came to be there, before realizing it was blindingly obvious. After all, who in our house was guilty of regularly nicking stuff and squirrelling it away? Yep, this secret stash had Winslet's pawmarks all over it…

"We're spying. New people!" said Tor, pointing towards the removal van.

It *was* quite exciting. It would be great if we got some friendly new neighbours, and you certainly couldn't describe the Fitzpatricks – who'd moved out the day before – as friendly, unless you started the word "friendly" with an "un" in front of it.

Grumpy old Mr and Mrs Fitzpatrick had lived next door for *hundreds* of years, getting older and grumpier as time went by, and I don't think anyone living round here was exactly heartbroken to see them leave Palace Heights Road for their new sheltered home. I know that sounds really mean, but *you* try living next door to people who *growl* at you when you go past.

"So who're our new neighbours, then, Tor?" I asked my brother.

"Not them," Tor replied, pointing to two guys in matching red boiler suits staggering out of the lorry with a long, black leather sofa.

"Well, I think I can figure out for myself that the removal men aren't moving in!" I grumbled, prodding Tor in the stomach and making him giggle.

It was then – thanks to being crouched down – that I spotted the edge of something sticking out of his trouser pocket.

"What's this?" I asked, grabbing it, then stopping dead when I realized it was the last photo Mum had sent of herself – from Canada this time.

I'd wondered where it had gone – I'd spotted that it was missing from the pinboard in the kitchen last week.

"It's just Mum," Tor shrugged, grabbing the snap back.

Aw, bless. That made me go kind of *churny* inside, thinking of Tor taking that photo and carrying it around with him. It was *so* sweet (and so sad too). Well, whatever *I* was feeling *he* was looking embarrassed, so I decided to talk about the new neighbours again to give him a chance to stop blushing.

"So apart from the delivery men," I starting chattering, "haven't you seen anyone else go in next door?"

"A big, tall man arrived," Tor whispered, shoving the picture back in his pocket. "He had an aquarium!"

Ah, so that was why Tor's radar was up. A fish fan moving in to No. 26 had his instant attention. I swear, a psychotic serial killer could move in next door, but if he had a hamster, Tor would immediately see him as a fellow pet-loving buddy. I could tell straight away that I was going to have to restrain Tor from trotting up to the front door and trying to wangle an invite to inspect the New Neighbour's pets and swap tales of fin-rot.

"OK, so we know there's a big, tall man and some fish moving in," I said, slapping my hands on my bended knees. "But what about gorgeous teenage-boy love gods? Seen any of *them* carrying suitcases inside?"

I was only fooling around, and fooling around with Tor is fun – he's always guaranteed to snigger at even my most rubbish jokes. But my blood ran cold when I heard someone else – *two* someone elses – sniggering at what I'd just said.

"Yeah? *You* should be so lucky!" Linn teased me, pulling the front door closed behind her. "If a – what was it? – oh yeah, 'love god' did move in next door, he sure wouldn't be looking at *you*, Ally!"

I could have handled Linn taking the mickey out of me – hey, as my big sister, it was part of her job – but I couldn't bear the fact that Alfie was standing by her side, grinning down at me.

What impression must I have given him, hunkered down beside the bushes in my school skirt, looking like I was having a *wee* or something, and wittering on about "love gods"? OK, let's just say that the phrase running through his mind wasn't "Mmm – Linn's sister is *so* fanciable! How come I never noticed before?".

"C'mon, Alfie – let's leave the kids to play in the bushes!" Linn grinned wickedly, yanking the creaky gate open and heading out on to the pavement.

"Sarcasm is a really pathetic way to get laughs, and you're only showing off in front of Alfie!" I stood up and shouted after her.

All right, that's a lie. I didn't.

But I wish I had, instead of staying crouched down exactly where I was, wishing that just for once, I could look like a reasonable sane, attractive person in front of Alfie, instead of a complete *dork*.

"Oh, by the way," Linn's voice suddenly hovered somewhere above me, along with a rustle of leaves as she parted the foliage to stare down at me. "Your boyfriend Billy phoned for you about five minutes ago."

"He is *not* my boy –"

…friend, I was going to protest, but Linn and Alfie had already wandered off, chattering amongst themselves, before I'd got the chance to finish.

"That's *it*!" I spluttered to myself, stomping irritably towards the front door and leaving Tor and Rolf to their detective duties.

"It" was basically fancying boys. And "it" seemed to lead to nothing but humiliation. Turning into a tongue-tied, bumbling geek with a brain of mush … getting caught drivelling on about "love gods" in front of Alfie … it was more than my fragile self-confidence could stand. There was only one thing I could do – from now on I was going to harden my heart towards Alfie (and any other random, second-division crushes I sometimes indulged in) and stick to boys as friends *only*. It was a lot less traumatic.

And anyway, apart from the humiliation, what boy could fancy me with my fat little jelly belly?

"Billy?" I bleated down the phone, desperate to hear a male voice that wasn't sniggering at my stupidness.

"Nyuh? Hewow? Aaawwwy?"

Luckily, I knew this language Billy was suddenly talking. Let me interpret: "Nyuh? Hewow? Aaawwwy?" translates as "Yeah? Hello? Ally?". The root of this ancient language is English, which is then mixed with a gob full of peanut-butter sandwich. It has no official name, but I like to call it "Pigface".

"Yeuchh!" I winced, holding the receiver away from my ear. "Billy, *don't* eat while you're on the phone to someone! It's totally disgusting!"

"Ung, sowwwy. Hoe on…"

(Translation: "Oh, sorry, hold on … I'm a total dweeb and don't deserve to have a friend as pretty and talented as you". OK – so I might have made the last bit up.)

It sounded like Billy had stepped away from the phone, hopefully to finish chewing however much sandwich he still had rammed in his mouth.

"Hi! How're you doing!" Billy said breezily after half a nano-second, which was a suspiciously short time for him to have chomped and swallowed. I had this horrible vision of him spitting half a mangled mouthful of bread and peanut butter into his hand so he could continue our conversation.

Bleurghhh…

"I'm all right," I shrugged, even though he couldn't see me hunch my shoulders. "So, what's going on?"

Normally when I ask him that, he'll say "Nothin'", or, if he's having a *really* wild day, "Not much".

But today – well, knock me down with a very large feather – something was going on. A *couple* of somethings, as I found out.

"Listen," he said, lowering his voice, "Mum and Dad are going out to a party tomorrow night, and I was thinking of getting a few mates around."

"Yeah?" I replied, perking up. "Like who?"

"Well, like Steven and Hassan and Richie. And you, of course. And your mates."

"What? All of them? Like Chloe and Jen and everyone?"

"No, not all of them," he hissed down the phone, obviously trying to keep the Saturday night mate-fest quiet from his folks. "Just maybe Sandie. And Kyra, course, since Richie's coming."

Hmm. Could be a laugh. Billy's school buddies Steven and Hassan were all right. Not cute or fanciable, I mean, but pretty funny sometimes. Yep – tomorrow could be kind of cool. A definite improvement on staying in and slagging off all the contestants on *Blind Date*, that was for sure.

"Right – I'll phone Sandie and Kyra and see if they fancy it," I replied, tangling the phone cord round in my fingers.

"Brilliant!" Billy responded, a bit too loud. Quick as a flash, he dropped his voice again. "Listen, if you bump in to my mum tomorrow during the day at the shops or anything, don't let on, yeah?"

As if I would. Billy's mum was really house-proud and pernickety (put a cup down on the table without a coaster and consider yourself never invited round again), and the idea of Billy having a noisy, potentially messy bunch of mates round without her there to oversee the proceedings (with a pair of rubber gloves on and a can of Pledge in her hand) was unthinkable.

"Sure," I nodded to the lavender-coloured hallway wall. "So what time should we come round?"

"About half-seven. Oh, and Ally – there's something else," he whispered so low that I had to press the phone right up to my ear.

"What?" I quizzed him, finding myself whispering too – who knows why, since the only pair of ears listening in to my end of the conversation belonged to a cat that wasn't Colin, who was gently snorey-purring through the bannisters behind me on the stairs.

"Can't tell you now – someone might be listening. Tell you when I see you tomorrow night."

"Aw, come on – that's not fair! You've got to give me a little clue at least!" I teased him. "Just whisper it!"

Hurrah – my whining worked. He gave me a clue all right – a great, big, fat one.

"OK," he hissed, sounding strangely wobbly. "It's just that I think … I think I'm in love!"

Billy in love? For real? For *real* real? Not just fancying someone?

Well, blow me down with a whole *bunch* of feathers. This was serious. And weird. Actually, hearing his news right there? That's how I felt – seriously weird…